Miss Highsmith's Adventure at Danford Hall

The Bellinghan Boys, Volume 1.5

Jeanne Johnson

Published by Jeanne Johnson, 2024.

This is a work of fiction. Similarities to real people, places, or events are entirely coincidental.

MISS HIGHSMITH'S ADVENTURE AT DANFORD HALL

First edition. May 17, 2024.

Copyright © 2024 Jeanne Johnson.

ISBN: 979-8224572632

Written by Jeanne Johnson.

Also by Jeanne Johnson

The Bellinghan Boys
Miss Clayton's Highwayman
Miss Highsmith's Adventure at Danford Hall

Miss Highsmith's Adventure at Danford Hall
Lincolnshire, England, 1814

Chapter 1

Emma Highsmith's Mama had been fussing all morning, but it wasn't until the whole family sat down to luncheon did they discover the cause of her distress. It came as a surprise for Emma to learn that she was the reason for her mother's disquiet. She'd made a living of trying to be as invisible to her mother as possible, leaving her younger sisters to bear the brunt of her Mama's scrutiny. Her sisters still had the chance to bloom into beautiful flowers, whereas she had accepted that at 25 her blooming days were over. She'd soon be a forgotten ornament on a dusty shelf, a spinster, alone in the world forever, but at least she'd be able to study her music in peace. Once her sisters were out in society they would be the ones forced to attend soirees and she could stay home to tinker on the pianoforte.

"An invitation!" Her mother flapped the crested paper aggressively at Emma, as if she had been responsible for penning it.

"To what Mama?"

"The Bellinghan summer ball, at Danford Hall!"

The way her mother was looking at her made Emma feel guilty. It was nonsense of course, she was not at fault. Besides, an invitation of this gravitas would normally have been met with jubilation, not anger. Really, her mother should be thanking her for maintaining a girlhood friendship with Mrs Hannah Bellinghan (or Hannah Clayton, as Emma had known her), not scolding her.

"I do not understand how this might cause such distress Mama. Surely it is a great honour to be remembered by such a well connected family?"

She glanced at her father for support, he shrugged and continued to attack his lunch.

"An honour extended to only three of us. Papa, myself and you."

Her mother placed particular venom on the word 'you', before sighing, "What about your sisters?"

Ah, there it is. Why invite the spinster when the marriageable prospects stay at home?

It hurt a little to know just how thoroughly her mother had given up on her. Emma bristled at the slight.

"Mrs Bellinghan was my particular friend as a girl," she offered, "perhaps she still thinks of Lucy and Catherine as children?"

At fifteen and sixteen years respectively, Emma also found it difficult to think of them any differently. Could she really have only been seventeen when she was first thrown to the marriage market?

"It is still a great honour," she finished weakly.

"Greater still for you, my dear," her father interjected, "for Mrs Bellinghan has asked you to join her as her house guest before the festivities."

That was a surprise, Emma and Hannah had not been in much contact for the past year.

"Me?" She squeaked at her mother.

Her Mama's face was like thunder. It seemed that she had not intended to mention that last piece of information.

"I've half a mind to refuse." Her mother huffed, "There's all kinds of rumours about that family. Not to mention that business with the Claytons and the highway robbery last year. Ten days alone with that crowd might ruin your chances of marriage entirely"

Emma grew frustrated. Ten days away from home sounded like bliss.

"I thought you said at my age that ship had sailed already Mama?"

"Do not be vulgar Emma." Her mother sniffed haughtily.

"If you do not believe the Bellinghans of Danford Hall to be worthy of our acquaintance, then you should refuse the invitation."

Her mother looked stumped. The Bellinghans were the richest family in the county, they could introduce the Highsmiths into social circles that they could only dream of. Despite some of the rumours surrounding the family, it would still be social suicide to refuse such an invitation, they all knew it.

Her father's voice cut cleanly across the table.

"You're going Emma. Have a lovely time. Mrs Bellinghan is to arrange a chaperone for you, so she clearly does not believe you are too over the hill."

"Mr Highsmith!" Her mother scolded, but he settled her down with a pat of his hand on hers.

"Your Mother and I will travel down the evening before the ball to dine with the family as Mrs Bellinghan has so generously offered. That is the end of this discussion." He glanced at his wife briefly before returning to his lunch. Whatever words had been forming on her mother's lips were swallowed, and she nodded her head curtly.

Emma smiled into her lap.

Over a week away from home and her Mama! A chance to reunite with Hannah, an opportunity for change...it was intoxicating! She desperately needed an escape from the monotonous timetable of her life. Although the ball was still several weeks away, Emma's excitement began to rise. It felt like the start of her own little adventure.

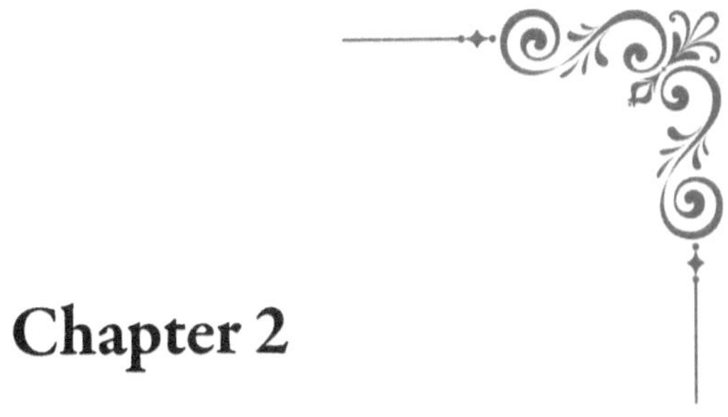

Chapter 2

The weeks couldn't pass soon enough.

What had started as excitement had soon turned sour as Emma's Mama fussed over outfits and etiquette. It seemed that her mother had no faith in her to behave in a ladylike manner. It was not as though she had never been out in company before, and yet her Mama seemed to think that without her careful scrutiny Emma would disgrace her whole family.

"You must sit up straight," she'd nag, "smile and converse. Do not sit there silent all week."

Emma would nod in appropriate places, but she had no intention of sitting quietly at Danford Hall.

Though she found conversing with strangers very difficult, there was more than one way to make noise at a private party. She'd daydream of the grand pianofortes that the great house would surely have, and amused herself by imagining the reactions when everyone realised that the slightly awkward friend of the hostess did have talent. Emma loved to play, she loved even more to compose. She felt the notes in her soul, as real as her own heartbeat. She could convey more meaning in one piece of music than she ever could in words.

Unfortunately, her Mama had little patience for noise, and saw no value in Emma's only talent. But she had no love of reading, horse riding or needlework. Her fingers itched to play, not to paint. When she was forbidden from touching the keys she found herself daydreaming melodies. The thousands of different combinations of sounds were as clear in her own mind as the endless chatter of her mother.

Hannah has written to say that there would only be her husband's family in attendance. Mr Bellinghan had three brothers all married. There would be no escaping the fact that she would have to speak to them all throughout her time at Danford. She hoped after a couple of days her anxiety would subside and she'd be able to open up. At least there would be no unmarried men present, she'd found them the most difficult to traverse during her seasons on the marriage mart. Most of the time she could barely choke out three words together, and none of the young men she had been introduced to seemed to have anything interesting to say. Though spinsterhood was far from an ideal situation, it would protect her from having to bear anymore unwanted scrutiny. And, as a spinster, it would be acceptable for her to stay all night at the pianoforte without being forced to converse with anyone. She wouldn't have to dance, sing or attempt witty conversation. That, to Emma, sounded like bliss.

The day of departure finally arrived, and with it a crest emblazoned carriage and four horses. Emma had hoped to see Hannah disembark, but instead a footman and a ladies maid came forth. Both were bearing letters, one for her parents and one for her. Emma had torn into its contents greedily. Hannah had written to say that she was much engaged with the ball preparations and could not travel herself today.

A stab of disappointment cut through her, though her Mama had sniffed like a snob at the news. Emma hardly felt slighted; her friend had sent four horses, two servants and the finest carriage Emma had ever seen. She was hardly roughing it.

After a few brief farewells to her family Miss Highsmith was on her way to Danford Hall at last. Her Mama, desperate to have the final word, had left her with some advice, "Speak well of your sisters Emma, you may yet secure them an invitation."

She had appeased her mother with a weak smile, but she had no intention of doing anything of the sort. This was her adventure afterall, and not theirs.

Enclosed in the luxurious interior of the carriage, Emma forced herself to meet the eyes of her chaperone. It was refreshing to be accompanied by someone so young, even so it took a moment for her to feel brave enough to speak.

"Lovely to meet you," she managed with a croak, "I'm Miss Highsmith." The words had formed incorrectly and sounded clunky to her ears, but she'd managed it at least.

The girl smiled back, seemingly unphased "Tilly, miss. I'm to be your dresser."

Emma had not considered that she would be able to make her own decisions on dress and hair whilst she was at the Hall, another splendid surprise!

"Mrs Bellinghan told me to pass on 'er apologies for not coming herself," continued Tilly, "she can hardly wait to see you again, she's been talking about you coming for some time." The girl thought for a second, "I think she wants a friend from home, to give 'er some support."

Emma frowned, at her questioning expression Tilly ploughed on.

"Don't mix my words Miss, she's doing a grand job. It's been so nice to finally have a mistress at the Hall! The place needed a woman's touch. Nah, she's just worried about the ball. It's a big job miss, sorting it all out. There's a lot of pressure on 'er to make it perfect."

Emma nodded bemused. Tilly's words seemed to gush out of her like a torrent, desperate to fill the carriage with as many sounds as possible. She hoped the girl would not be too disappointed with her introspective silence. She enjoyed hearing her pleasant chatter about Danford's new mistress. Of course Emma knew that Hannah would excel at running a house as fine as Danford, though it was concerning to hear that she was putting too much pressure on herself to make things perfect. Emma knew all too well that perfection was a dangerous thing to try and chase. She'd lost many hours to compositions while she'd tried to achieve that very same trait and knew it was an impossible feat. Nothing can be perfect. Perhaps Hannah felt pressure from other sources. Everyone knew that Mr Bellnghan's family were far wealthier and more connected than Hannah's had been. Many people considered his choice of bride odd, that he had marrying beneath his station. Perhaps she just wanted to prove some of the naysayers wrong? Emma would gladly offer her friend support if her endeavours were to prove the neighbourhood gossip wrong. After all, she knew all about feeling like an imposter, she felt like one in her own family! Her sisters were beautiful, confident and assured. They would fare much better on the marriage mart than she had. No, if Hannah felt an imposter then she'd do whatever she could to allay those concerns. Her friend was born to be mistress of Danford Hall, Emma just knew it.

Not long into her musings Emma realised that things had gone quiet in the opposite seat. She'd glanced across the carriage to see Tilly quietly snoring. A spike of joy rushed through her and she surprised herself by laughing aloud. For the first time in weeks she felt relaxed. She was free of her Mama for ten whole days, she could rise when she wanted, dress how she chose and play as much music as she could get away with. She could not wait for her adventure to begin!

HOURS LATER, EMMA CAUGHT her first glimpse of her friend's new home. Danford Hall was just as impressive as the gossip had made out. It sat like a beacon of pale limestone amongst the dazzling green gardens. Stately and awe-inspiring as Emma had never seen so big a residence before, she couldn't help but gawp.

Tilly woke with a snort as the horses pulled to a stop. "You ready Miss?" she asked, as though she had not been asleep for almost the entire journey.

Emma smiled nervously at her but nodded. She was glad that Tilly would be the one to take care of her for the next ten days.

The footman opened the carriage door, Emma took his hand and gingerly stepped out. Her legs ached after several hours of confinement. As she approached, the grand doors of Danford were thrown open and out strolled Hannah on the arm of her very handsome husband. Emma was suddenly twisted up with nerves. She did not want to disgrace her friend in front of her influential husband. She tried to remember her mother's advice, squared her shoulders and lifted her chin as she strode towards them in greeting.

"Emma," Hannah beamed at her friend, "thank you so much for coming."

Emma curtsied neatly, "Mrs Bellinghan, Mr Bellinghan. Thank you for your invitation."

"Any friend of Hannah's is welcome at Danford." Mr William Bellinghan replied with a polite bow. "How wonderful it is to see you again Miss Highsmith."

Emma had only met Mr Bellinghan a handful of times and felt the usual bite of discomfort when speaking to someone she hardly knew. But this was her friend's husband, she had to move past it quickly for Hannah's sake, she forced her mouth to speak, though they could all hear the shake in her voice.

"It is lovely to see you too sir. I hope you have been taking care of my friend?"

Hannah smiled at her with pride, knowing how difficult even that short speech may have been for Emma. Then she turned to glance at her beloved, and a look passed between husband and wife. They spoke a secret language to each other that Emma was excluded from. Her friend was radiant, flushed and joyful. Her husband gazed at her, openly affectionate. Together they made the perfect newly wedded couple.

To her surprise, Emma found herself feeling a little sad. Her friend had left her behind in her spinsterhood.

"He's been taking great care of me, I can assure you." Hannah beamed, then crossed to Emma and embraced her, "It is so good to have you here Em. Come, let me show you around."

Arm in arm the ladies walked into the great house, with an indulgent husband following behind in their wake.

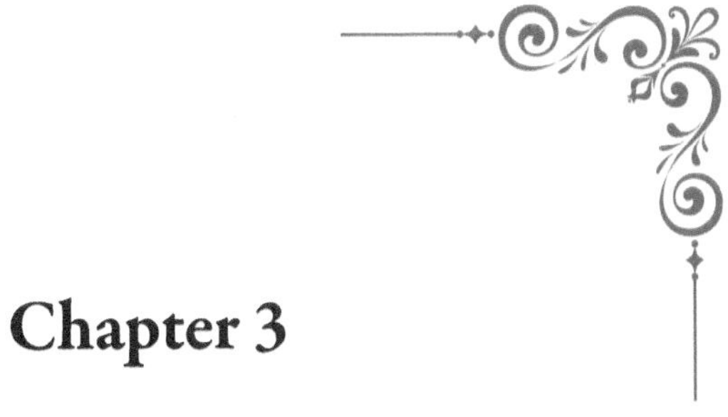

Chapter 3

The Hall's interiors were just as impressive as its facade. Emma felt her mouth salivate when she saw the pianoforte in the sitting room. It was the finest instrument she had ever seen; honey coloured mahogany with intricate inlaid flowers that crept up its squared legs like a field of wildflowers caught in a summer's breeze. The keys called to her in their siren song and she found it difficult to be torn away on the tour. But when she was shown into the music room, she almost choked. The pianoforte in there was not so ornate, but it was housed in an entirely separate area for practice. A room entirely dedicated to music, and one the occupants of the house could choose to stay in all day if they wished. Heaven! She wondered wistfully, as the tour continued, how long it would take her to summon up the courage to ask if she could use the space during her visit.

Rounding a corner Hannah spoke, "Are you ready to meet the rest of them?"

A knot of nerves twisted in Emma's stomach as the noise of playful chatter emanated out of the door they were standing before.

She felt her friend squeeze her hand. "They are not all assembled, Charles and Felicity won't be joining us for another day or so. They won't bite," she whispered.

"Much," muttered Mr Bellinghan.

This earned him a gentle nudge from his wife.

Emma smiled at this exchange, feeling herself relax a little. The people inside were all Bellinghans. If they were half as welcoming as the two people with her now, she didn't have anything to fear.

The first meeting is always the most anxious one, but she'd have almost two weeks to make their better acquaintances. She had to start somewhere.

Inclining her head in agreement she straightened her spine, squared her shoulders and followed her friend into the small gathering of people chatting merrily in an enormous drawing room.

As they drew nearer Emma felt three sets of eyes land on her. It might have halted her steps were it not for Hannah's encouraging hand at her elbow.

"May I introduce to you all, Miss Highsmith. Emma and I have known each other since we were children, she is our guest of honour." Hannah beamed.

Emma's throat went dry. The Bellinghan family all looked so vivacious and fashionable, she felt like a dullard in their presence.

First she was introduced to Mrs Charlotte Bellinghan and her husband Captain John Bellinghan. She understood he was the youngest of the four brothers, though there hardly seemed to be many years between them. He had a wry smile, a confident attitude and hazel eyes just like William. His wife, Charlotte, did not push Emma to speak, for which she was very grateful. She seemed the kind of woman who noticed everything, but kept her own counsel until action was needed.

Next Emma was led to a very glamorous looking blonde lady. She stood gracefully from the plush chair she had been lounging in and at full height she was at least a head taller than Emma. She wore an exquisite blue gown and an amused expression on her face as they bowed to each other. Emma felt herself shrink away.

"May I introduce Mrs Lydia Bellinghan. Lydia, this is Miss Emma Highsmith."

"For God's sake Hannah I know, I heard from where I was sitting." Lydia turned her powder blue eyes to Emma and scrutinised her carefully, "She's doing everything properly to impress you."

Mr Bellinghan stifled a laugh at his sister-in-law. "Couldn't you have played along for at least a moment? We are trying to pretend that we are a civilised family."

Lydia shrugged, "No point in deceiving the poor girl is there?" She gave Emma an austere glare, "Now then, it's best you become acquainted with my ways since I am to be your chaperone. We like plain talking, interesting stories and wine. I shall expect you to help me indulge in all three throughout our time together."

"Lydia!" Hannah chided whilst her husband laughed aloud.

Emma felt her cheeks burn at the news that Hannah would not be her companion. She knew her friend might be busy arranging the ball, but to be left in the care of a total stranger was a bitter pill to swallow.

She realised that Mrs Bellinghan was waiting for a response from her. Those blue eyes bore into hers expectantly, but her mind went blank.

"Indeed," she croaked eventually, detecting a hint of disappointment emanating from her chaperone.

Lydia looked stern, "You may call me Lydia, it'll make things easier with three Mrs Bellinghans in the house."

"If you are certain," Emma whispered and watched as Lydia rolled her eyes.

Things did not seem to be going well.

"You've got a peculiar look about you. Those big eyes in that pale little face." Catching Emma's blush she reiterated, "Peculiar in a fascinating way you understand Miss Highsmith. Fascinating and beguiling. Quite lovely." She pondered for a moment, glancing at the door as though in anticipation of someone, "You're not on the hunt for a husband are you?" she blurted out.

Emma spluttered. She'd only ever been subjected to such impertinent questioning from her own mother and was unsure how she was expected to respond.

"Lydia!" Hannah intervened, "That is enough. You are making Emma feel uncomfortable."

"I was only asking because of..." She paused, glanced again at the door and then changed tactics. "Perhaps, I can introduce her to some people at the ball." Lydia swept her arm around the room, "There'll be slim pickings of husband material in the run up I'm afraid my dear. If you are interested in that kind of thing."

Emma felt mortified, John Bellinghan looked away, embarrassed for her, but his wife held her gaze, silently entreating her to speak up.

"I'm not... I am not looking for a husband," she spluttered loudly. Her words cut through the huge room like a gong. Charlotte Bellinghan smiled slightly then looked away.

Her chaperone nodded approvingly too and moved to stand next to her, taking her arm. "Good girl," she whispered conspiratorially, "in most cases husbands are severely overrated. Take a turn with me about the room."

It hadn't been a request, Lydia began to move immediately dragging Emma along with her. Emma threw a final desperate look at Hannah over her shoulder. Her friend looked concerned for her, but did not intervene.

"I apologise if I made you feel uncomfortable, Miss Highsmith," Lydia demurred, "but as I said earlier I prefer plain talking and there is something that I must..."

At that moment the sitting room door opened and two men strode in mid-conversation. The first was unmistakably a Bellinghan, he shared the same sleek features as his brothers along with their fair hair and hazel eyes. The second was taller and quite a bit broader than his companion. In fact, there was something about his broad shoulders that made him seem so much bigger than the other men in the room.

He looked nothing like the other three, his eyes were a shocking blue and his hair a darker shade of blonde. His features were more rugged, a broader nose and lower brow, but then not all brothers shared a close resemblance and there were four Bellinghan brothers after all.

Lydia exhaled a sharp huff, "Too late," she murmured to Emma, before addressing the pair, "speaking of husband material!"

The men approached, the shorter of the two crossing over to Lydia and brushing a kiss onto her temple.

"Staying out of trouble I trust?" he asked before turning his eyes to Emma. He seemed to be assessing her in a similar way that Lydia had.

"Miss Highsmith," Lydia said, "my husband, Mr Henry Bellinghan."

Emma curtsied as the new Mr Bellinghan addressed her, "So you're the poor creature that's got to be shackled to my wife over the next week. I wish you luck Miss Highsmith." She smiled as he continued his assessment of her. "Look at those doe eyes, very striking, don't you think Dewsbury?"

She glanced up at the taller gentleman in surprise. Dewsbury? So he was not a Bellinghan after all? She found him striking in a rugged sort of way. Masculine, broad, toned, brutish even, as though he might burst through his cravat at any moment. Emma felt a deep pull inside, it was a jolt of desire so acute that she blushed. Very rarely did she find anyone physically attractive, and never to this extent on first meeting. It surprised her with its intensity. She found herself fascinated by his robust beauty, it was like staring at an expanse of churning ocean, powerful and alluring. However, it could not be any clearer that the gentleman did not reciprocate these emotions. As Emma glanced shyly up at him she was surprised to note that he was staring at Lydia with a look of undisguised rage on his face. She winced at the force of it, and she wondered what Lydia could have done to deserve such ire. His loathing seemed only heightened by his extraordinary physique, but Lydia was nonplussed.

"Allow me to introduce my cousin, Mr Dewsbury."

The introduction forced the two of them to meet each other's gaze, and though slightly better concealed his eyes were still aflame with rage. He glared at her as one might stare at a servant who had dropped a dish of hot soup in your lap. She felt her skin prickle defensively. How on earth could he be angry at her? What was her offence?

She bobbed automatically in greeting, but he barely deigned to nod his head at her. This irritated her even further.

"A pleasure to make your acquaintance Mr Dewsbury," she found herself saying, a little too forcefully. So many syllables for a man so displeased to meet her.

He cut her a curt nod, his eyes moving across the room to where Captain Bellinghan was standing with his wife.

"Miss Smith," he murmured in response without looking at her.

"It is Highsmith, sir," Emma replied automatically, surprising herself again with her ability to speak, "Miss Highsmith." Her voice did not shake at all, even after such a snub.

Lydia looked impressed. She had not thought this Highsmith girl to be in possession of a spine.

"Excuse me," was Mr Dewsbury's reply, and without a second glance he strode across the room to converse with the Captain.

Emma stood dumbstruck for a moment, staring at the space he had exited with her mouth ajar. If there had been a witty retort on her lips then it had surely died there unspoken. She had been thoroughly dismissed. On sight Mr Dewsbury had deemed her unworthy of conversation or even a single moment of his time.

Eventually Lydia snaked her arm back through hers and they resumed their jaunt around the room.

"I will not ask you to forgive my cousin's rudeness Miss Highsmith," she murmured, "he does not deserve it. I will not excuse his behaviour. He did not know that there would be any unmarried ladies here, but that is hardly your fault. In fact, it is mine, for I had completely forgotten that you were due to join us, else I would not have extended our invitation to include him. He has been staying with us for over three months due to...unforeseen circumstances. Will you forgive me? It'll make things much easier for us over the next two weeks if you do."

Emma replied in the affirmative, though she was still annoyed

"It would be best for everyone I think," Lydia continued, "if you were to just ignore him as much as feasible. He is tedious at the moment, for various reasons which I will not bore you with now. I do hope that he has not upset you?"

Emma shook her head, "No." But she knew that was a lie.

She was so tired of disappointing people just by the nature of her existence. He was angry because she was unmarried? Join the club sir, it had many vocal members. She did not need a reminder that it was too late for her.

Lydia drew them to a stop and turned to her charge, "If you had been interested in a husband, then I would not have recommended him as a candidate. Not in his present state, at least. There was a time when he might have been perfect for any young lady. Now though... "

Emma interjected, "I am not looking for a husband. As I said."

Lydia's eyes sparkled, "Excellent," she replied with a smile. "You know Miss Highsmith, I wasn't sure that you and I would get along together, but there is a hidden steel in you. I look forward to seeing more of that." A shy smile crept onto Emma's lips, at least she was getting somewhere with her chaperone.

"Come, let us find a glass of wine, and you can tell me all about Hannah as a grubby child."

That made Emma laugh, she turned back to look for her friend only to meet the icy gaze of Mr Dewsbury by the fireplace. Her smile died instantly, he turned quickly and she was forced to stare at the broad expanse of his back. Any attraction quickly turned sour, in fact a wave of dislike flooded her emotions as she looked upon him. Lydia was right, she was better off staying away from that one.

Chapter 4

The rest of the day passed in a blur of other people's conversations. Emma was not convinced that she had fulfilled Lydia's wish for interesting stories quite yet, but at least she'd been able to mutter more than one sentence to her chaperone over the passing hours. She'd had the rest of the tour of the house from Lydia and her husband while Hannah had been whisked away to attend some business. Emma would have felt more at ease with her friend present, but she was able to appear suitably impressed at the grand rooms and impressive furnishings, and there was little call for her to speak when Lydia and Henry bickered playfully with each other throughout the afternoon. They had toured the Hall for well over two hours before Henry had proposed seeing the gardens, and his wife had all but bit his head off at the suggestion. Reluctantly he'd conceded that it was almost time to dress for dinner, and as a compromise Lydia suggested a jaunt around the gardens culminating in a family picnic the next day. Emma was grateful for the delay, she'd completely lost her bearings and was beginning to feel a little fatigued. However, at the very least the tour had removed her from Mr Dewsbury's icy company for a while. He had quickly declined the offer to join them and had remained with the others in the drawing room.

Emma had been shown to her bedchamber, and after ringing the bell she was happy to greet Tilly again. The two of them set about dressing her for the first of many lavish dinners at Danford Hall.

"How was meeting the family Miss?" the girl had asked as she applied herself to taming the pile of chestnut frizz that had become Emma's hair.

She thought for a moment before responding, "Overwhelming."

"Ms Lydia can be quite overpowering," Tilly agreed, "but you'll get on fine with them all. Have no fear."

Emma nodded, but was not so convinced that she would ever get on well with Mr Dewsbury.

After what seemed like an age, Tilly completed her task and stood back impressed at her handiwork. Emma could not fault her for her pride, for she'd never looked better. Somehow the girl had managed to tame her frizz back into sleek ringlets and had even created a stylish twist at the back of her head. It really was most impressive.

AFTER ONLY GETTING lost once on the way downstairs, she had finally managed to locate the main corridor that led back to the sitting room where they would all meet before dinner. Unfortunately, she could also see the unmistakable frame of Mr Dewsbury up ahead of her and so slowed her steps so as to avoid having to walk with him. She'd needn't have worried, for although he almost certainly must have heard her footsteps, he did not look back and in fact widened his stride to put more distance between them. With his long stride in a matter of seconds he was gone. By the time that Emma had actually reached the sitting room, he was already conversing with Henry Bellinghan with a glass of wine in his hand, looking like he'd been there for hours. Inwardly Emma scowled. She hadn't wanted to walk with him, but what kind of gentleman sped up to purposely outpace her? Lydia was right, he really was tedious.

Unfortunately, given the size of the party, it would not be possible to avoid each other completely. As guest of honour she had been led into the dining hall with the Master of the house, but was seated at the table with Hannah on one side of her and Mr Dewsbury on the other. She could almost feel the icy chill emanating from his back throughout the whole meal, he'd turned away from her almost as soon as he'd sat down, choosing to converse with Henry and Charles and never turning her way at all.

That was not an issue for Emma, it meant she could speak to her friend all evening and the conversation flowed quite naturally when the two of them were together. It was just like being a girl again, Emma began to feel herself relax at last. By the fourth course the conversion had flowed, quite naturally, to the topic of marriage. This was not surprising, six of the eight people around the table were partners. In fact it had been Emma herself who had raised the topic to Hannah, she wanted to know how she was finding married life. Unfortunately, the subject soon spread, and eventually all the Bellinghan's were enraptured. Happily married people always had strong opinions on the topic of matrimony, this however placed both Emma and Mr Dewsbury into an awkward situation. As the only unmarried people around the table they were suddenly thrown into the lamplight.

"Come now Dewsbury," Captain Bellinghan had needled, "how much longer until we see you hitched? You can't tell me you're remodelling that house of yours for no reason. I know a nest builder when I see one."

The Bellinghan brothers all laughed, while Mr Dewsbury shifted in his seat, his huge shoulder brushed Emma's but he showed no indication that he'd felt it.

"Nonsense." He replied.

His tone implied amusement, but Emma could sense the tension radiating off him. She saw it in the set of his jaw, and how his smile never reached his eyes.

"The house remodelling is purely coincidental." His eyes glanced pleadingly to Lydia, who nodded but said nothing.

"But what sort of thing interests you in a lady Dewsbury? Who should we be introducing you to at the Ball?" Captain Bellinghan asked before his wife chided him for his impertinence.

Mr Dewsbury was now leaning away from the Captain as if to try to escape his questions. His shoulder pressed further into hers, she wished she could speak up to tell him to get back to his own place setting but she daren't. She wanted none of the attention from this particular line of enquiry to land on her, so put up with it for the time being. He felt very tense, like his bicep might burst through the seams of his jacket at any moment..

"He's interested in rank," replied Henry, seemingly to help his wife's cousin.

But Captain Beliinghan would not be deterred. "How dull," he snorted, "anything else?"

"If my cousin decides to marry then he would carefully choose an accomplished lady of breeding. No more, no less." Lydia replied, her tone implying very clearly that this was the end of the conversation. The Captain either did not pick up the hint or cared not to.

"Urgh," he scoffed, "Rank? That's what Will thought he wanted too. Now look at him. Have you ever seen a man so happy?" He shot a wink at Hannah before taking his own wife's hand and kissing it. "The heart wants what it wants in the end, Dewsbury. You'll see."

"Well, all mine wants at this moment is to be left alone." Mr Dewsbury replied. Emma felt the low rumble of his words through their brief contact. His tone hid the vast discomfort that was written throughout his taut body. Despite herself, Emma found she admired him for that skill; when she was uncomfortable she found it impossible to hide anything. She subtly moved her hand beneath the table to gently touch him at the elbow. She did it to make him aware of how close he was to her and allow him to move without drawing attention to it. He practically jumped out of his skin at her feather-light contact. Snapping his head around to look at her as he hastily shifted back to his proper place, he gave her the most withering look of disdain Emma had ever experienced in her entire life. A curious thing happened; she did not shrink away, she felt deeply irritated at his anger instead. In fact her cheeks were burning hot with it. She let out a small disgusted exhale and turned back to Hannah shaking her head slightly.

Hannah looked puzzled and Emma just rolled her eyes in annoyance. Fearing further discomfort Hannah rose from the table at that instant and the ladies retired quickly to the sitting room, much to Emma's relief.

As the others settled themselves with glasses of wine, Emma paced angrily near the pianoforte. Her fingers itched to explore the lovely instrument, she had not played for days now and she needed to get out this glut of emotions that were swirling inside. Hannah, conscious of her friend's discomfort, saw her and exclaimed, "Oh Emma, you must play for us."

The other ladies looked up at her expectantly. "She is a marvel," Hannah explained, " just wait and see."

Lydia did not look convinced, Emma felt her confidence falter as her blood pressure began to fall again.

"Don't want to disturb you," she murmured halfheartedly to the room in general.

"My dear," sighed her chaperone, "we will find a way to gossip whether there is music or not. Now play for us. It'd be a shame to waste such an expensive instrument, since none of the rest of us will perform."

She indicated the piano stool with a wave of her hand, Emma took her seat automatically. Who was she to argue with her chaperone?

Instantly, she felt the most at home that she had all day. Her trembling fingers carefully lifted the ornate lid. She was not nervous now, it was anticipation that made her hands shake. They settled on the keys like old friends meeting again, soon the music was flowing out of her as easily as breath. She read no manuscript, she played from memory alone, her eyes were trained down at her hands but they did not see. She was in a trance of muscle memory, entrenched in the song so thoroughly that even a storm ripping through the room would not have been able to stop her until she had reached the end of the movement.

Time stopped, it no longer held any meaning to her. Eventually she lifted her head, a smile perched on her lips, the song finished at last. She glanced up at the ladies and realised, for the first time, that the three of them were not talking after all but were all looking wide-eyed at her.

Had they been staring for the whole song? Emma had no idea. But soon the sound of applause ripped around the room led, most surprisingly, by Lydia Bellinghan.

"Well!" she gushed, "Aren't you a revelation Miss Highsmith?"

"You did all that from memory?" asked Charlotte, flabbergasted.

"I told you. I told you!" cried Hannah happily. "She's a marvel."

"Oh, play again." Charlotte begged, "It's been so long since we had proper music. We are all hopeless!"

Emma happily agreed.

A quarter of the way through the next piece, a noise did disturb her from her revelries. The door of the sitting room burst open and a voice warmed with brandy declared:

"I must see for myself which Bellinghan is the musical maestro, for I know such talent could not be my cousin..."

The rest of the sentence died on his lips as Mr Dewsbury found Emma at the keys.

He stared at her for a moment, almost as though he couldn't believe what he was seeing. His full attention on her made Emma pause and her fingers stopped automatically. He really did seem to fill the room. In Emma's eyes he loomed larger than any storm, and was equally as destructive to her piece of mind. It was not just his physical presence, but the mental space he took up. Wherever he was she was acutely aware of him. She hated that since this afternoon when they were first introduced, his hateful attitude towards her had been the thing to bring her out of her shell more than anything else. Now he stood before her, the full force of his stare bearing down with a spark of interest in those impossible blue eyes. Drat, she hadn't meant to notice his eyes. She could tell he was torn between anger and admiration. Emma stared back, frozen like a cornered animal, but defiant all the same. Her chin raised and she cocked an eyebrow. The message was very clear: *Go on. Say something.*

Lydia grinned at her in admiration.

Dewsbury cleared his throat, "Do not let me disturb you Miss Highsmith."

"A little late for that, I rather think." She replied crisply, surprising herself, Mr Dewsbury and all the Bellinghan wives.

He bowed awkwardly before taking a seat in the furthest possible chair from the pianoforte.

Emma continued with a renewed fervour and an invigorated flush to her pale cheeks. She played for well over an hour.

The whole time Mr Dewsbury sat quietly drinking. He did not look over at the instrument at all, but he spoke to none, enraptured by the music for the rest of the evening.

Chapter 5

Emma slept well that night, the musical itch having been scratched thoroughly and to great applause no less. It felt good to have surprised them all, and she could now default to the piano stool when she felt overwhelmed by the conversation. She worried at not being witty enough to keep up with the trio of Bellinghan wives currently present. She did not read much, and so failed utterly to engage in the lively conversations about novels she'd never heard of. She was certain she could feel Lydia's eyerolls at her stilted attempts at responses, even if she had not directly seen them. With the impending arrival of a fourth Mrs Bellinghan later that morning, Emma was concerned that she would just melt away into the background like some forgotten ornament. The men would be out all day hunting, not that any of them gave her much mind outside of their own conversations. Each Bellinghan brother seemed completely devoted to his wife. If the brothers were not conversing with each other then they seemed content to speak with their spouse. Mr Dewsbury kept to himself mostly, though spent some time with Lydia and Henry between bouts of broody silence. None of this left much room for Emma. She wished she had the confidence to open up immediately. She found that time and trust were key to her eventually slipping out of her well maintained shell, neither of which you were granted when introduced to new people at a social engagement. Her mother had long given up trying to introduce her to strangers.

Mr Dewsbury's rudeness still loomed large in her mind. Being slighted by him had hurt, and yet it had manifested an odd thing- that she had been forced into anger and by proxy some of her real self had snuck through in her brief interactions with him. Small things, but noteworthy by her standards. She had been struck with the thought that if not for his dislike vexing her greatly, then she did not think that she would have dared find the pianoforte that evening. She'd been too worried at making a spectacle, of seeming desperate for attention. She'd intended to raise the suggestion of her playing for the party after a few days had passed and she had settled in with the company more. Instead his rebuff at the dinner table had wound her up to the point that she had to seek the keys to vent her frustrations. It was curious just how much he had affected her in their brief and frosty acquaintance. She had spent a great deal of last night thinking of his cold reception to her. She wondered what today would bring.

Tilly dressed her expertly at seven thirty and so by eight she was already walking the corridor eagerly awaiting breakfast as she always did. Music and breakfast were two of Emma Highsmith's very favourite things. Rounding a corner she stopped abruptly as she met Mr Dewsbury at the top of the stairs about to go down. He looked up automatically upon hearing her approach but quickly averted his gaze. She imagined he was stuck between wanting to leave, and realising that there was no way that he could pretend not to have seen her. Emma narrowed her eyes and approached him slowly. She'd be hanged if she would greet him first. Politeness be damned, he'd shown her no politeness yesterday at all and she could return the favour. She was going to ignore him, walk straight past him down the stairs and hope that the back of her head would haunt him the same way his had haunted her yesterday.

For some reason though he waited for her.

"Miss Highsmith," he murmured as she drew level with him, "good morning."

No bow, Emma noted, so she did not curtsy. It felt odd to openly flout the expected routine of politeness so early in the morning. She did not reply, not because she could not find the words, but because she did not care to. That also felt oddly freeing.

She descended the stairs expecting him to stay where he was, but instead he matched her pace and they walked the steps together in silence. At the foot of the staircase she was certain that he would take his leave of her and divert himself to a different corridor, but he did not. Emma's heart was pounding. It rattled in her chest like a clanging bell, not out of desire or some other foolish feeling, but rather out of anxiety. She was so afraid that he would point out her effrontery and she'd been shamed in her friend's new home. Mr Dewsbury did not attempt to say anything more, he did not leave her side, but did not offer her his arm as they strolled towards the breakfast hall. The silence was broken only by the clip of their footsteps on the wooden floors. When at last they had arrived at the breakfast hall, Emma felt as though an eternity had passed. Mr Dewbury arrived at the door first and paused for a second whilst he reached for the handle. Emma tried to force herself to speak, but found she had no words afterall.

He opened the door for her and waited for her to pass. "Enjoy your breakfast," he said.

His voice was surprisingly soft for such a big man, she was almost ready to forgive him some of his effrontery from the day before, but then he turned and fled down the corridor they had just walked, leaving her to eat alone.

Emma found herself as relieved at his behaviour as she was annoyed. He had left her to eat alone in a very ungentlemanly gesture, and yet had accompanied her all the way here. He had somehow managed to be both courteous and rude to her, all before 9am.

EMMA ENJOYED A HEARTY breakfast alone, until around half past nine at which point she was finally joined by Lydia and Henry Bellinghan.

"Good Lord," exclaimed Lydia as she approached the table, "up already Miss Highsmith? You'll have to get out of that habit over the next week. We shall have to keep you up later."

"You can't chain her to the pianoforte all evening my dear," her husband replied deadpan as he took a seat next to Emma.

Perhaps it was the two plates of food she'd lovingly consumed that made her bold, but she found herself replying, "Honestly, I think I'd love that. I'd feel less pressure to try and be witty."

Lydia and Henry both looked at her in surprise and then laughed.

"My dear Emma," Lydia replied, "I swear every time you speak you surprise me greatly, and in the best possible way I assure you." She leant in conspiratorially, "Perhaps, just try and speak a little more?"

"Lydia." Her husband warned.

She held her hands up in surrender, "I'll say no more. Now where's that wretched cousin of mine? I swear he said he'd be down first and you know how early he rises." She rolled her eyes and her husband shrugged.

"He accompanied me to the breakfast hall, but did not stay to eat." Emma replied, surprising everyone.

Henry glanced at her, and then at Lydia, "He did not join you?"

Emma shook her head and watched as Lydia narrowed her eyes.

"Insufferable," she hissed quietly, then reached to take Emma's hand, "I hope you have not been too long on your own this morning. I shall be having words with him, this is not to be borne."

"Pray, do not mention it." Emma replied, squeezing her hand, "I am unbothered, as you can see. And besides, if he had stayed, I cannot imagine what we could have possibly spoken about."

Lydia smiled, though it did not reach her eyes. If anything she looked a little sad. "You see, you surprised me again." She sucked in a deep breath and shook her head, "There's only so many excuses I can make for him, but he knows how to behave like a gentleman and chooses not to. He used to be a decent fellow before…" she stopped herself quickly. "No matter," she indicated to her husband with a nod of her head, "they'll all be out hunting once Charles and Felicity get here. I'll just pray that his horse unseats him into a patch of nettles."

That brought a smile to Emma's lips, despite her best efforts to conceal it.

UNFORTUNATELY THE WEATHER had other ideas. By ten, as Hannah and William finally emerged for breakfast, the sky grew dark, at half past they all heard the first rolls of thunder and by eleven the heavens had well and truly opened. The rain had even scared Mr Dewsbury out of his hiding spot and he joined them all in the sitting room for tea. Standing gloomily by the window as the rain lashed the panes, he stared out angrily at the clouds. His tea cup looked comically dainty in his large hand, as though it had been spun out of sugar and that he might take a bite out of it at any moment. Emma noticed all these things as she sat near the mantel on the other side of the room. She found her eyes could not stop searching for him at any given moment. It was as though he was a great viper in the room and she had to always know where he was lest he strike.

Lydia had immediately accosted him once he'd joined up with the party. Emma had watched silently as she'd taken him to one side and spoken, quietly but animatedly, to him in the far corner of the room. It was odd to think that she was the matter under discussion. She had tried to not stare through the duration of the chat, not wanting to be accused of orchestrating the reprimand. But Mr Dewsbury never once looked over at her. He'd taken his scolding in stride then secreted himself by the window, where he still remained. He'd make no move to apologise to her, that seemed obvious. Lydia had described him as being a decent man once. Emma had to wonder what had changed him. But then, rich men may do as they pleased in this world, she supposed. Then the idea struck that she did not know for certain that he was rich. She had just supposed, given that he was Lydia's cousin, that he must be a man of means, but really what did she know about him? He was remodelling his home. Well, potentially only rich men could do that, though he had been staying with Henry and Lydia for over three months, so perhaps he was hard up after all. He was unmarried, that she knew for certain. He was an unmarried man who had engaged in lengthy home renovations that had possibly run him dry. That really wasn't a lot to go on. He was tall, broad and handsome. Emma blinked. Oh. She wasn't supposed to still notice that he was handsome. Besides, it was an odd sort of attractiveness; angular, rugged, not the sort of thing that she'd ever been interested in before. Not there had ever been a 'before'. She tore her eyes away. She'd done too much supposing already this morning.

By eleven thirty the new Bellinghans had arrived, cold and shivering. After an initial soggy introduction they went to change before joining the party proper. Charles and Felicity Bellinghan seemed as amiable as the rest of them. Charles and Will looked very much alike, with the exception that Charles had very green eyes compared to his other brothers. Felicity was so delicate and beautiful she looked almost breakable, but she was as warm as Hannah and as caring as Charlotte. Suddenly there was a lot of chatter in the room as the family fell back into an established rhythm of conversation. Both Emma and Dewsbury found themselves at the fringes of conversation. It was clear the family had been apart for some time and had much that they wanted to catch up on. Emma did not begrudge them this, and so quietly slipped back into muteness, occupying herself instead with mentally tinkering over a new composition that had crept into her mind over breakfast. The notes were bombastic but melancholy, and she was having some problems in figuring them out. She was unsure how much time had passed before she realised that Mr Dewsbury had joined her. He was silently looming by the arm of her chair, his tea things abandoned on the mantelpiece beside them. She glanced up at him cautiously, but he was not looking at her, preferring to stare into the main body of the room where the various Bellinghans held their conversations. He did not seem upset at being excluded from their chatter, though she wondered why he had removed himself from his quiet spot by the window. He certainly did not seem interested in striking up a conversation with her. They could barely hear the rain now over the noise of the company, but it steadfastly rolled down the panes signalling an end to the proposed hunt and tour of the gardens. Perhaps the disappointment of their cancelled plans had made him move? There was a palpable air of disappointment that surrounded Dewsbury wherever he went. Though, that may have been Emma's own prejudice against him talking. Lydia had mentioned, more than once, that he was usually a decent person, Emma supposed that something must have happened recently to change that. She could not imagine Lydia extending this invitation to include her cousin if she'd known that he would behave in such a way. His behaviour mortified Lydia greatly, his refusal to engage with anyone in the party for more than a few moments before slipping back into his brooding solitude was a source of embarrassment for her. Emma suspected that he might be receiving more than one scolding from his cousin before the week was out.

With their outdoor activities cancelled, the suggestion was made to play cards to pass the time. The idea was met with much jubilation, even Emma felt enthused as she fancied herself fairly good at cards. Mr Dewsbury, however, refused the invitation to play, Even after it was pointed out to him that his lack of participation would leave someone (namely Emma, though her name was never directly mentioned) unable to join in due to the odd numbers, he still did not relent.

To save being further drawn into it Emma had attempted to back out also, proposing that she could be at the pianoforte instead. Hannah refused this, she had been insistent since William and herself would be absent most of the afternoon on party planning business that Emma should play and the family would take it in turns to sit a hand out. She was an indulgent hostess, but even so, her voice betrayed some annoyance at Mr Dewsbury's selfishness.

Emma was annoyed too as she found herself sitting opposite Captain Bellinghan and the cards were being shuffled. Not because it was the younger Mr Bellinghan that she was partnered with, but the fact that, despite his unwillingness to play, Mr Dewsbury did not excuse himself from the room. He stayed close, like a looming shadow at her back for most of the afternoon.

Chapter 6

The rain continued all night. By breakfast the next day it was agreed that the excursion around the grounds had to be postponed to at least the day after next in the hopes of the paths being dry enough to traverse. That meant another day of being trapped indoors. Emma paid no mind to this, she was used to staying inside and she rarely got to stay in such luxurious surroundings. The men seemed despondent at their hunt being delayed again, and Hannah glanced nervously at the rain spattered window panes as though the clouds had been sent by her local critics to try and ruin her ball.

The party spent the day at the card tables again to pass the time. The men, being unaccustomed to confinement, bid too high and played too competitively with each other. All except Mr Dewsbury of course, who absconded soon after luncheon and could not be found again. Nobody protested his absence, not after yesterday, besides the Bellinghans were having too much of a good time together. Emma tried and failed to come out of her shell, but found the gay group to be so overwhelmingly familiar with each other that it almost left no room for shy interlopers to inject themselves into their conversations. For the most part she was happy to listen to their stories, managing to speak a few words when directed to answer, but she was unhappy at her lack of progress with her interactions with the family. She worried that she was an embarrassment to her friend. Eventually melancholy clouded her mood and she'd asked to be excused from the sitting room, feigning a headache.

She meant to return to her bedchamber, but she felt her fingers begin to itch. She needed to play, to pour her emotions into her music, to express herself in a way that her words were failing to currently. This nagging new melody begged for development, it filled her mind with potential passages. If she could only find the music room. She knew she would feel better having worked on the tune at the keys. Maybe it would settle her nerves and she'd be able to converse with the others over dinner. Desperately trying to recall the house tour from days before, she tried and failed twice to find it; discovering instead the billiards room and a silver closet.

By the third door she was fairly confident that she got it right. Stepping confidently into the darkened room, she groped around for a moment confused by the lack of light. Marching to the covered window she threw back the curtains only to discover that she was not in the music room after all. She had instead discovered a private library... and Mr Dewsbury's hiding spot.

Of course, of course! Only he would have purposely drawn the curtains to stew in the dark like some cave bear. He'd squinted up from a leather armchair, surprised by the sudden rush of light and that his solitude had been disturbed. Then, on discovering who had stumbled into his fortress of gloom he scowled. He held a brandy glass in his right hand, a half empty decanter of the golden liquid sat on an end table next to him. That told Emma everything she needed to know. She scowled right back. She would not curtsey, even though every sinew of muscle was screaming at her that she must, but she would not give him the satisfaction.

He did not stand, he drank instead, those cold blue eyes assessing her from across the room. She froze under the scrutiny, unable to move and unwilling to speak.

"Miss Highsmith," he murmured, his voice thick with drink, "how fortuitous that it should be you to find my little hiding spot. But then

I bet your Mama will have taught you how to seek out unmarried gentlemen, much like a bloodhound."

In two days this was the most words he had ever spoken to her, as ungracious as they may have been.

"I did not..." she began, but he cut her off.

"All the same. All the same. Just so happened to be passing by were you? With those pretty little accomplishments, a compliment here, a dance there. This one's got intellect, she'd sweet talk the Pope into giving her what she wanted." It occurred to Emma that he barely even registered that she was there. He was no longer looking at her, choosing to wince into the light of the window instead.

"This one's a musical maestro, smouldering brown eyes to lure the bait. Ridiculous. Who has eyes that big?"

Was he referring to her? She could not be sure.

"Sir, I..."

But he rambled on, "Well I'm no trout Miss Highsmith. I won't be caught. No fine net to reel me in." He was almost incoherent now, his tongue seemed too big for his mouth and the smell of brandy burned off his breath like dragon fire. He finally snapped those startling blue eyes back at Emma. "There is no husband material in here for you," he concluded moodily.

Stung but rattled now, Emma felt her timidness crack, "That sir, is abundantly clear."

Her words filled the space between them as crisp as the morning breeze. She thought she heard him gag on his retort, but she was out of the room faster than he could form the words.

Drunken oaf! How dare he insinuate that she would orchestrate an opportunity to be alone with him after his affrontary over the past two days. The gentleman must have a ridiculously high opinion of himself if he believed her to be in any way interested in seducing him.

"What an ass!" she hissed to herself, relishing in the forbidden pleasure at having sworn aloud.

After that disastrous meeting, she decided that she did in fact have a headache, and went to lay down in her room before meeting up with the rest of the party for dinner.

At the banquet table that evening, Mr Dewsbury had the good grace to appear to be suffering from his afternoon over indulgences. Mercifully he had been seated away from Emma at the table that evening, and the two of them did a good job of pretending that the other did not exist.

Afterwards, Emma had been persuaded by the Bellinghans to play once again, and was rewarded with great applause. She felt her spirits lift as her fingers finally touched the keys, and what she could not say over dinner she conveyed now with notes instead.

Mr Dewsbury said nothing to anyone for the rest of the evening, and excused himself from the musical performance at the earliest possible moment. Emma watched him leave with renewed annoyance.

THE NEXT MORNING, EMMA had risen early again. Half afraid that she would run into Dewsbury in the corridor, she'd peered cautiously around first, straining to hear any footsteps before exiting her room. She did not run into him. In fact she didn't hear or see anything of him until around luncheon when she had accidentally stumbled upon him and Lydia conversing in the drawing room. Emma hadn't meant to eavesdrop. She'd only walked that way to retrieve her shawl, which she had left after yesterday's great card gambit. But when she'd heard her name mentioned quite distinctly she paused and lingered by the door.

It was Lydia's wry tone, and she sounded annoyed.

"...to Miss Highsmith. You're behaving abominably James. I will not stand for it."

James, his first name was James. Emma blushed at this intimate knowledge, she knew she should move away, but found she could not.

"You can accuse me of nothing Lydia." She heard him reply rather defensively.

"I couldn't have said it better myself," Lydia snapped. "Nothing, you have done nothing. You have not contributed to the party in any way, besides moping and insulting Miss Highsmith by purposefully ignoring her more than anyone else. Everyone in the party can see it. Everyone is talking about it. It is not to be borne."

"I simply do not want her to get the wrong impression." Even through the door Emma could hear the frustration in his tone rise.

"The only impression that she could have possibly made," Lydia hissed, "is that you are a rude oaf. Which is an accurate one. For Christ's sake James, she is not interested in marrying. Not you, nor anyone, she told me this herself before you were even introduced! You do not have to be so cold towards her."

"And yet," he replied sharply, "she is constantly thrust at me. At dinner, at cards, at breakfast. All your fault of course, it was you after all who first introduced me to her as husband material."

"Have you gone mad cousin? You sat together once at dinner, and, on seeing your behaviour to her oldest friend, our gracious host has not sat you together since!"

"At cards then." He huffed.

"You refused to play!"

"We were roomed near each other."

"In the guest wing, as you are both guests! And may I remind you that you are the uninvited party here, not Miss Highsmith."

Emma heard him sigh heavily as he changed tack, "Tell me Lydia, exactly what mastery of wit am I missing out on? She sits there trembling like a little mouse until you provoke her to speak. She forces out three words of a strangled reply, those big brown eyes trembling with fear the whole time before she returns to silence. The only time I have ever seen her animated is when she is sitting at the pianoforte. So tell me cousin, what difference would it make if I turned my attention to her? Let me be, to do as I see fit for my own wellbeing."

Lydia launched into her defence with gusto, but Emma did not wait around to hear it. She had heard enough. A little mouse? That stung. Though she suspected that she did not make a good first impression, hearing it confirmed aloud by another was a hard thing to swallow. She felt tears burn in her eyes, but she would not let them fall. She hastened her steps and fled to her bedchamber to compose herself.

A mouse? The gall of the man who stands in the corners of rooms, like some spectre at the feast, speaking to almost no one. Now she had time to think, her upset quickly turned to anger. She paced the room, wild with indignation. How dare he? How *dare* he! When she had done nothing to him. Her crime, in his eyes, had been to be present at a party that he was also attending. And yet, she had been personally invited by her particular friend, whilst his invitation had been extended to him through his cousin. A formality only offered to him because he happened to be staying at her house. He was the unwanted creature, not Emma.

She was trying her best to come out of her shell, whilst he chose to stay silent and sulk alone in dark rooms instead. The cheek of the man!

Emma let out a frustrated growl. Hateful, hateful man. How dare he speak of her in such a way? He saw himself so superior to her, when really he was behaving much worse than she. Her fingers twitched with anger, they longed to play, to bash out her emotions against the keys. But Emma had too much respect for the beautiful instruments at Danford Hall than to subject them to that bruising. Besides, she had to rejoin the ladies in the sitting room soon before they sent out a search party for her.

She stood before the mirror to check her expression and took a deep breath. Her skin was unusually flushed and her brown eyes were alive with fire. Her hands refused to be still and she kept flexing her fingers. A mouse? She looked more like a wild cat, ready to pounce. She bared her teeth at her reflection before marching out of the room.

Emma arrived breathless back with the others a few moments later. Lydia had rejoined her sisters-in-law and the three of them looked up as she strode back into the room.

"Miss Highsmith, did you find your shawl?" Felicity asked.

Emma shook her head, "It's not in my room," she said, hoping to excuse her shortness of breath for distance travelled rather than level of rage. "I am certain it will turn up."

"You are so flushed," Lydia replied, looking concerned. She also had a heightened expression, no doubt from her animated discussion with her cousin. "Come, sit by me and drink some wine."

Emma had to laugh, it was barely past midday. The sound took them all by surprise, as did Emma's jovial response as she sat down next to her chaperone on the silk settee, "Oh yes, why not."

Lydia eyed her curiously, but still poured her a generous white wine from a carafe on the end table. "Capital." she murmured, as she passed Emma the glass. "You two will join us I hope?"

Felicity and Charlotte Bellinghan smiled wearily, but nodded all the same.

Emma's eyes toured the room properly, "Was Hannah called away again?" she asked after taking a large fortifying gulp.

Charlotte nodded, "She extended her apologise to you Miss Highsmith. I know she was very much hoping to spend more time with you these first few days, but the storm has added some complications to the Ball arrangements."

Emma waved her words away. "She's nothing to apologise for. And please, all of you, call me Emma."

Lydia's eyes sparkled, "I'll cheer to that!"

With the second burst of unexpected laughter that afternoon, Emma clinked glasses with the others, and felt herself finally let go and relax.

Three glasses later and the four women were giggling like children. Emma had been speaking about her sisters and the conversation had flowed quite organically onto their own siblings.

"Brothers are an immense bother," Felicity said forcefully, "especially when it comes to suitors."

"Did they give Charles a hard time?" Emma asked cheekily.

Felicity grimaced, "You don't know the half of it."

"Only trying to protect your virtue my dear, from that wicked Bellinghan second son upstart," Lydia drawled, "they didn't know it was already too late."

Emma choked on her mouthful of wine as the Bellinghan wives shrieked.

"And what about you?" Charlotte asked Lydia, her voice still holding some semblance of sobriety, "what was your excuse?"

Lydia shrugged, "I'm an only child."

The others laughed as the sitting room door opened and Mr Dewsbury walked in. Emma straightened her spine instinctively, the sight of him made her bristle with anger.

On seeing only the ladies he stopped mid stride. "My apologies," he said to them all as his eyes swept the room, "on hearing the laughter I had assumed the gentlemen were with you."

Lydia scoffed, "Because we couldn't possibly be having a wonderful time without them."

Dewsbury ignored her, "Where might I find your husband, cousin?"

"How the devil should I know?" she replied coolly, while refilling her glass. "He'll be amusing himself somewhere."

He glanced around the room again, this time counting wine glasses, "I see you ladies have found a pleasant way of waiting out the storm."

Charlotte smirked, her cheeks flush, "Oh, I think we gave up being ladies about an hour ago Mr Dewsbury."

"That's right," Lydia cried, "no ladies in here anymore, just creatures of the enlightenment with a thirst for knowledge."

"A deep thirst." Felicity mumbled and Emma laughed quietly.

Mr Dewsbury caught her eye, he seemed to struggle for a moment, no doubt thinking of the conversation he'd had earlier with his cousin. Eventually he addressed her, "Do not let these Bellinghans lead you astray Miss Highsmith."

His tone was light, an olive branch perhaps after his telling off from Lydia, but Emma was annoyed nevertheless. How dare he try and engage with her now, after two days of coldness, and presume to tell her what to do.

Her brown eyes met his unflinchingly, "As Lydia said, there are no ladies in here, nor any gentlemen either." She paused for a moment and enjoyed Lydia's admiration at her subtle insult. "The gentlemen are playing billiards I believe. As for myself, I am but a creature bound to obey my chaperon." She picked up her glass, and said, "A little mouse perhaps?" before taking a hearty sip.

She heard Lydia gasp as Dewsbury's face registered her remark, recognising his own words from earlier. He had the good grace to look ashamed, and whatever remark he might have made dried on his lips, unsaid.

"The billiards room is down the corridor on the right, I believe sir," Emma prompted.

With a stiff bow the big man hastened his retreat from the room without another word.

The three Bellinghan wives gazed at her for a moment in acclaim.

Lydia raised her glass, "Emma Highsmith, welcome to Danford Hall!"

Emma grinned as the four of them clinked their glasses together with a cheer.

Chapter 7

Emma woke the next day the happiest she had felt at Danford Hall. The assembly had passed a very pleasant evening chatting and playing cards, all of which Emma had participated in without unease. She had declined wine over dinner, opting instead to let the effects of the afternoon wine carry her newly found confidence into the evening. Once she found herself sobering it was gratifying to realise that her confidence did not shrink. She felt at home with the crowd at last. Well, almost all of them. Mr Dewsbury avoided her all evening, and she made no effort to engage him in conversation.

She rose later than usual and made no rush to change. If she'd learnt anything about these Bellinghans then it was that none of them were early risers. She did not feel afraid to run into Dewsbury alone, nor would she be ashamed (as she had felt earlier in the week) to purposely snub him. However, since she had no wish to pass another isolated breakfast, she chose to ready herself at a more appropriate Bellinghan time.

She met Hannah and William as they were entering the breakfast hall.

"Oh, this rain is worrying me." Hannah pouted, "What if it persists over the next week? How on earth will the grounds cope with all those carriages?"

Will kissed his wife's temple, "It will stop," he assured. "All will be well."

Hannah smiled weakly, but Emma could see the concern written there. Her friend was determined to show the neighbourhood that, despite her humble lineage, Will had made the right choice of bride. In her mind, everything had to be perfect, boggy driveways and muddy dance floors were not in her vision of perfection.

Emma took her friend's arm and gave it a reassuring squeeze, "All will be well." she repeated, and prayed that it would be so, for Hannah's sake.

After around half an hour the whole Bellinghan clan had emerged from their slumber. Some of them were looking a little worse for wear after the indulgences of yesterday. Namely Lydia and Felicity who only drank water over breakfast with their hands clasped over their eyes.

"Delicate creatures," Charlotte Bellinghan whispered, as she tucked into an enormous plate of food.

Dewsbury was the only person who did not arrive. Emma presumed he had eaten hours earlier, he tended to rise at around seven, then hated that she knew that.

She turned to Will, "I had hoped I may use the music room today, if that is acceptable?"

He smiled at her confident tone, "I am sure the instruments will be overjoyed as neglected as they are."

"Thank you sir, I may need to be shown the way. I tend to get rather lost in your wonderful home."

He nodded, "Of course, 'll have a housemaid take you after breakfast "

Emma thanked him again before turning to Lydia, "Will my chaperone be joining me?"

If looks could kill then Emma would be obliterated. "I'm sure you're capable of maintaining your virtue without me for just one afternoon. I shall be returning to bed."

Emma had to laugh.

An hour later she was sitting alone in the music room, her fingers itching with anticipation. Her most recent composition was stuck in her head, she needed to hear it played in order to iron out the kinks. There was something puzzling about this particular melody that she just could not put her finger on. The complexities of it had made sleep difficult last night.

She tried the notes on the keys. The bombastic grandness of them sounded exactly as she had imagined, but it did not suit the piece somehow. She tried again, loud and aggressive, the sound filling the room to the brim. But again, it was not right. She paused and thought. Perhaps there should be an air of melancholy? She tried again, the bold notes now quiet, slow, thoughtful. Yes, that was better. It seemed more honest.

The sound of the door opening disturbed her musings and the sight of Mr Dewsbury poking his head around the frame took her out of composing entirely.

"It's you." she said flatly, but without any particular reason, it had just sprung to her lips and escaped before she could stop herself.

Rather surprisingly he bowed, "Miss Highsmith. May I join you?"

Emma stared at him. Purposely placing himself in her company unchaperoned, even when he thought her a fortune hungry marriage trap? What was going on?

She must have nodded, for he entered the room and placed himself at the end of the pianoforte. How was she ever going to compose with him standing right there?

"What is it that you are working on?" he asked.

Encouraging conversation now, very curious.

"It is my own composition," she replied, not taking her eyes off him. More notes came to her as she stared, she longed to play them, but controlled her fingers for the time being.

"Remarkable. What a talent you have."

A compliment. Emma felt her head beginning to swim. What on earth did he want from her?

"Do you play Mr Dewsbury?"

He nodded, "Though nothing compared to you Miss Highsmith."

A silence fell between them. It felt as wide as the ocean. His little compliment seemed to bounce around the silent room, alien and awkward. She continued to stare at him and he cast his gaze at the wall. The longer she looked at him the more notes fell into place in her composition. She longed to try them out, but he was still standing there at the end of the instrument like some sentry. It irritated her, she wanted to play, alone preferably. Her frustration rose and provoked her to ask, "May I speak freely Mr Dewsbury?"

It surprised him enough to look back at her and nod.

"Why are you here? You have certainly never sought to maintain my company before."

He reeled from her words, embarrassed at the harsh truth of them, surprised that she had been forthright enough to say it so abruptly. "Yes. I came to apologise. And to hear you play as I did not have the pleasure last evening."

"Apologise?" Emma's voice betrayed her incredulity.

He nodded and looked at his hands, "I strongly suspect that you overheard part of a conversation yesterday in which I spoke about you in very ungenerous terms. I make no excuses for my rudeness, I should never have spoken about you in such a way, even in private. It is not becoming a gentleman, I apologise." He looked up again, to gauge her reaction. So far she had offered none. "I should also apologise for the state you discovered me in that day in the library while I'm at it," he added, "I can hardly recall what I said to you, but I am certain it cannot have been polite and for that I am sorry."

Emma did not blink, "Is that all?"

This seemed to surprise him. "All?"

"I admit to having felt some anger at overhearing myself being described as a witless mouse. Though, I must confess, my own mother has called me worse to my face, so you will have to do better than that if you wish to upset me."

"I did not wish to upset you. It was unfortunate that you happened to hear that part of the conversation."

"Unfortunate indeed!" she scoffed, "My goodness sir, if I held high hopes for this apology then you are certainly not meeting them."

He ran a hand through his hair, she watched the movement carefully and the music in her head seemed to scream.

"You're right," he granted, "what would you like me to say? I truly am very sorry."

"I had hoped that you would apologise for your behaviour from our first introduction." She tinkered a few notes on the keys while she spoke, her fingers refusing to stay still a moment longer. "That, I would say, has been your biggest crime."

Dewsbury huffed at her impertinence at forcing him to confront all of his actions, but knew he had no leg to stand on.

"Have you any interest in hearing my excuses as to why I was not pleased at meeting you in the first instance? I will gladly recount them all to you if you wish."

Her playing became more assertive, "No. I have no interest in excuses."

"Then I shall offer none."

"Good." she replied, slamming her fingers through a final chord. "Anything else to add sir?"

He looked annoyed, but somehow his eyes were dancing with mirth at their gentle sparring, "I apologise," he conceded, "I am sorry for how I have behaved. It is not the actions of a gentleman towards a lady of his acquaintance, you deserve better."

"And is it likely to continue?" she asked calmly.

"Not a minute longer," he replied.

On hearing the words pass his lips Emma smiled and inclined her head in a nod. There. A truce. She couldn't believe that she had spoken so boldly to him. Her own mirth fed into the notes, and soon enough the new melody flowed out of her easily, as though she were reading sheet music.

Dewsbury listened intently with his eyes closed, Emma couldn't help but watch him from her seat.

"That is really extraordinary Mis Highsmith."

"It has been rattling around in my head for the past few days." She tinkled the melody quietly as she spoke, not needing to look down at the keys to play it.

"Where on earth do you get the inspiration from?"

Emma shrugged, "It is just a feeling, a thought. Inspiration can strike at any moment."

"And what is the inspiration for this particular piece?"

"It's so hard to tell. This one has only just emerged over the past few days at Danford." She paused for a moment to think. She looked at Dewsbury's imposing frame, square jaw and blue eyes. She thought of his air of disappointment, his muscles taut with tension and brooding stare. Very suddenly everything clicked into place and she realised, "Oh, it's you."

She blushed, she hadn't meant to admit that aloud.

Dewsbury looked confused, "Me? What is?"

Emma cleared her throat, "I hadn't actually realised...this song is yours."

"Oh," he looked surprised, "play it again?" he asked gently, and moved a chair so he could sit by her at the keys.

Emma suddenly became very nervous at his close proximity. She seemed so acutely aware of him on her left that she doubted if her fingers would work the keys properly on that hand. It was one thing to play Beethoven to the assembled party after their evening dinner, but to play a self composed melody to the person who is the inspiration for the piece when they are sat mere inches away from you, was a completely different thing entirely.

She reached for the keys and saw her fingers tremble, but let the music flow as honestly as she could. It was a sad piece, slow and melancholy despite the grandness of the chords she had chosen. There were moments of anger, clashing harmonies and duelling tempos, but always it returned to a quiet sadness that underpinned the whole composition. By the end she was quite embarrassed. Yesterday she had overheard Mr Dewsbury speaking to someone honestly about what he thought about her, but now she had just shown him, in the most intimate and detailed way possible, what it was she thought about him. It felt like baring her soul, and she did not like it. She also did not care for the lingering silence that was left behind as the final notes faded away.

Dewsbury furrowed his brow, "I see," he said, leaning back in his chair. "Yes. I see. How enlightening."

Emma swallowed, her embarrassment burnt on her cheeks, "I d-did not mean...it does not mean anything, just a silly composition. Still rough, needs lots of work, obviously," she stammered.

"Do not distress yourself Miss Highsmith. I am certain that you have been kinder in your assessment of me than I deserve." To her surprise he moved, and seated himself next to her on the piano stool, "Here, who do you think this is?"

He tinkered with some notes before settling on a simple tune. It was bolshy and playful. Droll almost in its languid tempo.

Emma had to smile, "Lydia!" She laughed as Dewsbury nodded. "I would have added more power," she replied, glad for any distraction from her own piece.

Her hands joined his at the keys, fingers winding their way adeptly around his to the keys she sought. Together they composed a rough approximation of her chaperone in musical form. It was fun. Funny even. The melody they made was scarily accurate and Emma found herself laughing as the notes filled the room. Dewsbury's shoulders began to relax, his features were less tense, his eyes less brooding. He did not smile, but it was a welcome relief from the icy tension that had marred their acquaintance so far. Emma felt herself light up inside.

"What's this commotion then?" Lydia's voice asked from the doorway.

Dewsbury shot up from the pianoforte like he'd been stung. He tried to cover his movements by offering Lydia a small bow, but it was blatantly obvious where he'd been sitting. Two unmarried people alone in a room unchaperoned, it could cause quite a scandal. If it got out, Emma's reputation would be ruined. Not that she gave that any mind. She had as little care for the marriage market as Lydia did for music.

"Playing around with a duet, to dazzle you all this evening," Dewsbury replied smoothly.

Emma caught his eye with a questioning look, "I did not realise that we would be presenting a duet to the assembly."

Dewsbury's eyes danced merrily, "I will try my best to keep up with you and not be an embarrassment. To you too, cousin."

Lydia watched them both carefully, "How wonderful to see you two getting along James."

"Long overdue, I know," he replied with a shrug.

"Indeed," she muttered through her teeth. "Well, I shall very much look forward to hearing you both play this evening. Hannah has suggested dancing tonight, to celebrate the rain finally stopping. We may finally get our picnic in the grounds tomorrow Emma."

"How lovely!"

Dewsbury still towered over the pianoforte, his size only exaggerated as she sat and he stood so close.

"I will leave you Miss Highsmith, I have already taken up too much of your practice time." He turned and bowed to her, catching her eye in the process, "Thank you for my lesson. I shall not forget what you've taught me."

Emma stared at those impossibly blue eyes. Which lesson was he referring to? She had no idea. "Of course sir. Anytime."

He nodded and in five long strides was out of the room.

Now alone with her chaperone's questioning glare, Emma simply shrugged, unsure what to say.

Lydia groaned and rubbed her eyes, "I can't even begin to question whatever that was. I am going back to bed."

And that was the end of that.

Chapter 8

That evening there was dancing. Everybody seemed as amazed at Dewsbury's transformation as Emma had been. He spoke all evening, never once drifting off to lurk alone in a far corner of the room. He even brought his own sheet music, and the two of them sat down together to play a duet, much to the delight of the party. Afterwards, the tables and settees were pushed aside in the sitting room to make space for a dance floor. The Bellinghans laughed together as they swapped partners to dance, music and joy filled the room for most of the evening.

These Bellinghans knew how to enjoy each other's company. Emma and Dewsbury were both content to watch, not wanting to intrude on the family's precious time together. Emma stayed at the piano, the unofficial music director of the evening, and Dewsbury stayed by her side turning pages when required. Eventually, the Bellinghans grew tired of swapping partners and Hannah had cajoled Dewsbury onto the make-shift dance floor. Being the hostess, he could hardly refuse, though his body language betrayed some reluctance to move from the piano. Emma watched them quietly from over the lid of the instrument. She thought he moved very gracefully for such a big man. Hannah's hand in his seemed impossibly small, and yet he handled her as gently as porcelain. She watched him beam at some comment Hannah had made. His face lit up like a beacon, as though whatever burden he carried with him internally was forgotten for just a second. He looked younger somehow. He'd always been handsome, even when brooding, but that smile betrayed a beauty that Emma didn't know was possible in a man. All this from a small grin; one he had shared with their hostess. A lump formed in Emma's throat, she looked down guiltily at her busy hands. She felt the blood rush to her cheeks as shame burnt through her chest. Just for a moment she had felt jealous of her friend, and she wasn't at all comfortable with what that might mean..

AT NOON THE NEXT DAY, the party assembled at the foot of the grand staircase to finally embark on their tour of the grounds. The culmination of their grand tour would be a great picnic on the open lawns near the lake. After two days of solid rainfall Emma had doubted that this excursion would happen, but once the rain stopped and the sun came out Hannah had seemed determined. Now that emergency rain planning was no longer necessary she could finally spend some quality time with her friend.

Emma had bumped into Mr Dewsbury in the corridor of the guest wing and felt flustered. She had been running late, Tilly's fault for insisting on resetting her hair to look better in a bonnet. To save time she had rushed out of her chamber with the blasted bonnet in hand before Tilly could fuss around any longer with her curls. She had almost collided with Dewsbury in the hallway, too busy with tying her ribbon than to look where she was walking.

"Forgive me sir," she had gushed, her cheeks flaming red as she felt his big hand grab her elbow to steady her, "I did not notice you there."

His blue eyes crinkled with merriment as he indicated his whole form with a wave of his hand, "That is not something that I usually hear."

True, he seemed even larger than life to Emma at that moment. They were in a more enclosed space than usual, plus he was already wearing his tophat, which gave him at least another ten inches of height. Her burning cheeks also made her more acutely aware of his presence, suddenly the air inside seemed stiflingly hot.

Her words fumbled in her mouth, "You are usually very hard to miss."

She regretted her choice almost immediately.

Dewsbury on the other hand seemed delighted. The corners of his mouth curved, though she could not yet describe it as a smile. "Is that so Miss Hightsmith? I would have thought with your doe-like eyes you would have superior lines of sight." He offered her his arm, after a moment of hesitation she took it with shaking fingers. He seemed to have become fixated with her eyes, but then they were her one distinguishing feature.

"I only meant that I was not paying attention sir. Otherwise, obviously, I would have noticed you standing there," she was babbling now. For his part, Dewsbury let her go on as he towed her down the corridor. "You are positively Herculean in stature. Very easy to spot normally, even when you do not wish to be observed, as you tower over everyone. Besides, my eyes are not that big."

His eyebrows shot up, "Herculean? Tower over? You make me sound like a statue."

"Well there have been evenings this past few days in which, you must admit, you have lurked in corners like some gargoyle."

"Gargoyle? Things have gotten worse in a short amount of time!" Dewsbury's tone betrayed his mirth despite her insult, though Emma's head was still reeling. Why can't she just be quiet?. "But what if I told you, you doe eyed creature, that I would be a Duke one day, surely then you would go back to describing me as Herculean. I think I liked that description better."

Oh god. A Duke? He would inherit a Dukedom? Why on earth hadn't Lydia warned her against insulting future members of the peerage? Some chaperone she was turning out to be. She tried to bury her nerves, but she'd completely lost her head, "Duke or no, unless I see you do something heroic then you shall remain a gargoyle. And I do not count turning the pages for me at the pianoforte. I could have done that on my own."

Dewsbury lifted his hand in surrender, "Forgive me Miss for my intrusion on your great talent. I shall know better next time."

They rounded the corner that led to the landing.

Emma breathed properly for the first time since running into him and gained control of herself, "Please ignore me Mr Dewsbury. I had not meant to run into you this afternoon and I've no idea what I am saying."

He laughed then, an honest to goodness laugh that stopped them both in their stride at the top of the stairs. He turned his head to look at her, his face beaming, "My goodness Miss Highsmith, I don't believe that for a second."

The force of the joy in his astonishing eyes made her grip his arm more tightly. Her face melted into a broad smile. She wanted to drown in that warm ocean of blue.

"Ah there you both are," called a masculine voice from the foot of the stairs. The whole Bellinghan clan, clad in riding gear, looked up at them from the ground floor. Their eyes were gleaming.

Emma's stomach dropped. Riding? No one had said anything about riding! Or had they? Lydia had made a joke about habits at breakfast, but Emma had been too distracted by Dewsbury's conversation about Beethoven to really pay attention. She felt a deep sense of embarrassment as she realised that she did not want to have to admit in front of him that she was hopeless on a horse. She had one talent and one only, in all other accomplishments that a lady may have she was utterly useless. Shame burnt itself to the back of her throat but she admonished herself harshly. It would only matter if she was trying to impress him, but she was not. She was practically a spinster, it was too late for her to fall in love, and Mr Dewsbury was interested in a bride with breeding, something she also did not possess. Therefore, she reasoned, it mattered little that she would be forced to admit that she was no great horsewoman.

Sensing her tension Dewsbury asked her if everything was alright.

"I am not strong on a horse," she replied, and was proud at how little her voice cracked, "I had not realised that we would be riding today."

Dewsbury gave an unreadable, "Ah," and offered no more.

"I can see you do not intend to race the others," Lydia called to Emma as they drew near, "You've not even put a hat pin in that bonnet. It'd fly straight off!"

"Lord," said Emma, dropping Dewsbury's arm as they reached the bottom on the stairs, "today of all days you decide to take chaperoning seriously."

Surprised laughter rippled around the group, Dewsbury gazed down at her impressed. Emma felt her confidence return somewhat.

"I did not realise that we would be riding this afternoon. I'm afraid I have no riding habit with me. I..." she faltered just for a moment and sought Hannah's face in the crowd, "I am not a confident rider."

Hannah came to her, looped her arm through her friend's and led her away from Dewsbury, "We've picked out a lovely tempered mare for you. She's a gentle old soul who knows these grounds better than Will. She has not reached above a trot in years according to the stable master. She'll do all the work for you."

Emma still felt nervous, "Well I..."

"Miss Highsmith could ride with me," Dewsbury cut in, surprising everyone, not least Emma once she realised he had followed after her. The four Bellinghan wives exchanged questioning glances.

Emma flushed pink at the suggestion. The idea of being pressed against his chest, his arms draped around her for the duration of the afternoon made her head swim.

"N-no!" she exclaimed a little too forcefully. Dewsbury turned at her vehemence against his suggestion. "I could not. It is too much of an imposition."

"It is no imposition, it was my suggestion." Dewsbury replied smoothly. He studied her carefully, though she could not imagine what he was so curious about.

"Thank you sir, but my answer is no."

A beat of silence passed as the two of them stared at each other. None of the Bellinghans knew what to interject, staying silent as they witnessed the curious exchange.

Dewsbury looked both bemused and irritated at her refusal. Nodding his head in defeat he suggested, "Perhaps I could accompany you with a lead rope instead?"

"Capital idea James!" Lydia added excitedly. "You wouldn't object to that would you Emma?"

Emma shook her head, though she suspected that Lyda wasn't giving her much of a choice. "Charlotte and I can keep pace with you. We weren't planning on racing like the rest of them. We four can travel together whilst the others tear about."

Emma smiled nervously as Hanah led her outside. She really did hate being on horses. A lead rope was a useful compromise. It meant separate horses at least, and there was less chance of her being thrown by her mare. Today she would put on a brave face, even if it meant being led around the park on a lead rope like a child on a pony.

Swallowing her embarrassment she addressed the group, "That's very generous. Thank you."

SHIFTING HER WEIGHT on the side saddle for the eighth time, Emma desperately tried to remember her lessons from years ago. Her mother had long given up on her eldest daughter distinguishing herself as a strong horsewoman, and it had been agreed upon by all that the lessons were better spent on her sister Catherine who showed strong aptitude for the skill. By the age of nineteen it had become abundantly clear to Emma's Mama that her eldest daughter would not be enticing some wealthy man with a country house into marriage, therefore lessons on horse riding were an unnecessary expense. Her current mount: 'Hera', was as gentle and unphased as Hannah had suggested. Hera didn't seem phased by Emma's nervousness or her shifting weight as she struggled to find her centre of balance. It was Dewsbury, riding on her left with the guide rope in his hand, who seemed to flinch in alarm at her every movement. Lydia and Charlotte rode steadily ahead of them, chatting easily together as they explored at a gentle trot. The rest of the party had torn away under a thunder of hooves almost as soon as they were all mounted.

"Those Bellinghans are very competitive." Dewsbury had murmured to her, though there had been a hint of disapproval in his voice. He'd seen how nervous the sudden spurring of the horses had made Emma.

He leant over to her now, "Try to relax, Hera knows what she's doing."

Emma smiled weakly, so he tried another tack, "You have lived in Lincolnshire your whole life I understand Miss Highsmith?"

"Yes. All except for one season," she shuddered at the thought. Her introductory season in London had been a harrowing and humiliating experience. She'd been grateful when her mother declared that she was not worth the expense of attempting a second year in town.

"It is a remarkable county," he exclaimed, "I've never seen such rich farmland. It seems to stretch on into eternity."

Emma laughed, she'd never thought of it like that, "Where do you call home Mr Dewsbury?"

"Derbyshire is Dewsbury county. Lydia and I both grew up not far from Matlock. My home is further east from there now. It is called The Elms."

"You have commissioned lots of work on it I have heard?"

Dewsbury looked away, uncomfortable for the first time on this line of enquiry, "Indeed, the interiors are being remodelled in a more modern style," he paused, in thought for a moment. "I dare say it'll be done by now."

He didn't seem excited by the prospect, if anything his shoulders stooped at the thought, though he quickly shook it off. "It is not The Elms that should interest you though Miss Highsmith."

"Is it not?" she asked, confused.

"When my uncle dies Stancomb Hall will pass to me, along with the Dukedom of course. Title and property all in a neat little package. Most people are very interested in that." He sounded bitter, and his face betrayed tension again.

"Oh," she replied, unsure of what to say. "Until you mentioned it earlier I had no idea about that."

This seemed to surprise him, "Had not Lydia mentioned it?"

Emma laughed, "Her conversation rarely includes mentions of you. Except to berate your behaviour of course."

"Then she..." he paused, searching for the correct words, "She has not imparted to you the reason for my prolonged visit at her residence."

Curious now, Emma replied, "It was my understanding that this was due to the ongoing work at The Elms."

"And no one else has mentioned anything? Your friend, our hostess for example..."

"If Hannah knows any additional information then she has not shared it with me." Emma's tone was sharp, instinctively defensive of her friend, "She is not a gossip."

Dewsbury raised a hand in defence, "I would not dream of dishonouring her with the title. Especially since she has been so good as to accommodate my unexpected presence at her family gathering." He paused for a moment in contemplation. "She has done very well, your friend. And Will, Mr Bellinghan, he loves her dearly, anyone can see that. She need not be so concerned, I'm sure the ball will be spectacular with her at the helm."

Emma shook her head, which he caught out of the corner of his eye. "Did I say something amiss?"

She sighed in irritation, "You've no idea the pressure she is under. The whole thing, everything, has to go flawlessly. She is being scrutinised by every high born family in the county who wanted to join their names with the Bellinghan wealth. Everyone knew, everyone, that the Bellinghan heir was expected to marry into the aristocracy. Nothing less would do for the mistress of Danford Hall. And now they will find anything, any reason at all to disparage my friend. This is her first major test, and it is the final ball of the summer, the biggest private ball held in the country, the most sought after invitation of the social calendar and she is entirely responsible for ensuring it lives up to its reputation." She turned those big brown eyes towards him, forgetting, in her ire, that she was on horseback, and unable to keep the sarcasm out of her voice, "But I suppose you must be right, she need not be so concerned."

Abashed but shaken off guard, Dewsbury found that all he could do was laugh in surprise. "My goodness Miss Highsmith," he replied, "you have admonished me thoroughly. I am beginning to miss those days when you were too nervous to speak."

"Ah, I see them up ahead at last," Lydia cried from over her shoulder.

Somehow they had covered half of their journey and were arriving at the picnic spot. Emma had barely any time to notice her uneasiness on horseback, not when there was lecturing Dewsbury about her friend's virtues to be done.

They caught up with the rest of the party without another word. The others looked flushed from their race; hearts pounding, their eyes alive. Each Bellinghan brother dismounted easily and went to their wife to help them from the saddle. It seemed like a seamless ritual, a practice that was well trod and organic.

"Miss Highsmith?" Dewsbury's voice prompted. She turned to her left to see him standing next to her horse, his hand outstretched. She'd been too busy observing the others to notice that he had dismounted. She felt heat rise to her cheeks as his big hands curled around her waist. Leaning forward she released her reins and draped her hands either side of his neck. His arms lifted her like she weighed nothing at all, though she felt the strain in his muscles as he pulled her up and brought her body in towards his chest. Emma's pulse quickened. Her body was so close to his that she could feel the warmth of his skin. She had never been so close to a man before, not even her own father. She slid down his front as he set her gently on her feet. The whole movement had lasted only a couple of seconds but it has affected her deeply. She found that she was breathing heavily, and felt a deep yearning ache from between her legs. Mr Dewsbury showed no such signs of exertion. Lifting her off the horse had not been difficult at all. Though Emma noticed that he did not move away from her, nor extend the distance between them as propriety would dictate he should. He turned so his front was no longer pressed against hers, but they were still shoulder to shoulder. She could feel the taunt muscles of his arm leant against her. He felt solid and sturdy, not unlike a statue, beneath his finely woven clothes.

"Thank you," she whispered, her cheeks burning.

"A herculean feat you could say Miss Highsmith?" he teased, his eyes glancing briefly across her face, recognising her flush and seeming pleased at what he saw.

"Not quite," she quipped, and marvelled at the smile that broke across his face.

He offered her his arm, "Hungry?"

"Ravenous," she replied as she took it. Though ravenous for what she dared not imagine.

Chapter 9

"Oh, how the children would have loved this," sighed Felicity Bellinghan as she bit into another sugared biscuit. The sun shone a joyful yellow warmth onto the happy party as they lounged on blankets and silk cushions strewn across the lawn.

Charles kissed his wife's forehead fondly, "The seven of them together would have needed an army of nannies my love. We would have had no peace at all."

Emma choked on her lemonade, Dewsbury passed her a napkin. "Seven?" she asked incredulously.

Lydia laughed, "Not all Felicity's my dear. There's currently seven little Bellinghan's between us all."

"Though, there is always room for more!" Felicity replied, catching Hannah's eye and winking. Hannah smiled down at her lap where her husband's head lounged happily.

"We will, keep that in mind," she replied with a grin.

Emma smiled too. She'd never seen her friend so content. She ached with joy at her married bliss. it was more than either of them could have ever expected. Even as young girls they had both been pragmatic about marriage. Hannah had no dowry and her family had been in immense debt after her father died. Emma had a modest dowry but no charm nor beauty to catch a young man's eye. They had long acknowledged that if either of them were to marry then it would be an economic arrangement rather than an emotional one. Hannah would need to marry whoever would want to house her, and Emma would marry whoever would want her father's money. Now Hannah had married for love and Emma was about to become a spinster. How things had changed.

"How do you feel about children Mr Dewsbury?" asked Charlotte Bellinghan innocently.

He seemed taken aback by the question, almost choking on his own drink. "Well, Lydia's boys are awful. They've tormented me everyday for months now."

Henry Bellinghan laughed, "You shouldn't be so entertaining for them then James,"

Emma found her interest peaked, "You are good with children Mr Dewsbury?" she asked as she passed him back his napkin.

He shrugged modestly, "Those boys are just fascinated by their giant house guest."

"They will miss you when you return to Derbyshire," Lydia stated over the rim of her glass. "They have enjoyed your company immensely."

Dewsbury smiled, but offered no reply. Instead he turned back to Emma, "And what of you Miss Highsmith, are you good with children?"

Emma considered her answer for a moment, "I have not had much recent experience I'll admit. I was nine when my sister was born, but I forget much of those years now. I will endeavour to dust off my skills and be an indulgent aunt. It is as all aunts should be, I think."

"An aunt?" Dewsbury asked quietly.

Emma shrugged, "My family gave up on the idea that I would have my own children long ago."

Dewsbury's face remained impassive, though his eyes betrayed some surprise, perhaps even some anger at her revelation.

There was no time to dwell on it though, as the party soon made ready to continue with their tour of the park.

Mr Dewsbury lifted her back onto the saddle with the ease of a seasoned groomsman, though his hands seemed to linger on her waist for a beat too long. They rode companionably for the remains of the day, both enraptured by mental images of the other with a chubby cheeked baby cradled in their arms.

DESPITE EMMA'S RESERVATIONS about horse riding it had been a very pleasant afternoon . The combined effort of both Hera, who really was a gentle old soul, and Mr Dewsbury meant that by the time they were on their return journey Emma felt quite at ease. Even if Hera had spooked, which Emma doubted would ever happen, she knew that Dewsbury would be right at her heel to catch her. His steadfast presence had been both a comfort and a distraction. She couldn't help but imagine what riding with him on his horse might have felt like. Better not to dwell. Though that was easier said than done when he reached up to help her dismount one final time. The Bellinghan groom stood there looking completely redundant, a knowing glint in his eye. There really was no reason why Dewsbury had to help her himself now they were back at the stables. She slid down his front as he lowered her gently. Her hands rested at his collar, her fingertips brushing against a soft curl of dark blonde hair that fell by his ear. She blushed at the sensation, her hands were bare as she had neglected to re-don her gloves after the picnic. She liked the way his hands gripped her ribcage, she liked the way her breath caught in her throat, how his arms lifted her with seemingly no effort to place her back on the ground.

She thanked him briefly, embarrassed at the catch in her voice. They really should not be still standing so close together. She felt the warm pressure of his leg against her hip and a deep longing throbbed through her from between her own thighs.

"Lord, cousin," cried Lydia merrily as she approached them, "I think you must have caught the sun, your cheeks are so flushed."

Dewsbury stepped away from both ladies with a tight smile. Emma bit back a feeling of disappointment as he removed himself from her. Head swimming with a sea of emotion; frustration, confusion, anger, longing crashing together. It was all becoming too much! Her fingers twitched, she needed to play, to bash out her feelings on the keys in a cacophony of discordant harmonies.

Murmuring her excuses she removed herself quickly from the cousins before Lydia could say anything more.

Chapter 10

Propriety be damned, Emma practically burst into the music room as though it was her own private quarters. Struggling with the buttons of her duck-egg blue spencer jacket, she eventually flung the oppressive garment onto the piano lid. The day had been warm, but she felt stifled by the tight sleeves and high collar more than she ought. It was Dewsbury of course, he was the one who made her skin burn more intimately than the sun ever could. She whipped off her bonnet and it quickly joined the jacket in a heap. She sighed as she sat and opened the lid with restless fingers. They found the keys immediately and she crashed her frustration out wildly. As suspected, it was discordant and loud. It took her 5 minutes to realise that she was playing a frantic version of her own Dewsbury composition. Her cheeks glowed with embarrassment. It was humiliating how much her body reacted to him, how the simplest touch had made her knees weak and her insides throb. She couldn't help but ask herself, why now? Why him? Why! She had never been interested in a man before, why would her heart betray her now when she was four months away from spinsterhood and no man in his right mind would even look at her. She had been content to slip away into a quiet corner of the ballroom and let her sisters have the light that their Mama was so desperate to shine on them. They were young, gay, charming, with pretty accomplishments and bold natures. They would make good matches, marry, have sweet chubby children on whom Emma could dote. And Emma would have had no regrets. She could say that she tried at society, she'd failed to come out of her shell, but she'd given it a go. How could she regret it when she'd found no one she could open up to, no one she'd miss, no one who distracted her or that occupied her thoughts day and night?

That was until Danford Hall.

Now she would have to live with regrets. Mr Dewsbury was an inheritance away from a Dukedom. He was not currently seeking marriage. In fact he had told her, to her face, that he was not interested in her that day in the library. She recalled his words now as a mantra, "There's no husband material in here for you."

When he finally became interested in a marriage partner, it was an accomplished lady of breeding that he sought. That's what Lydia had said at dinner that day, he wanted rank, not a timid composer way past her prime. Tears pricked her eyes and she stopped to brush them away. In the silent pause between notes she heard her own breathing, as deep and frantic as the music had been. She put her hands to her face and leant into the steady strength of the pianoforte. Her elbows hit a selection of keys that formed a jarring chord which summed up her emotions perfectly.

"Enough," she told herself aloud.

Taking a deep breath she stood and gently closed the lid. Scooping up her belongings she began to make her way down the corridor with the intention of ordering a hot bath and hiding in her room for the rest of the evening.

She was not six feet down the corridor before she passed a door propped open with a large stack of books. The curtains had been opened this time so she could clearly see Dewsbury sat in his hiding place. Seeing him sat in that very same leather armchair made her stop and stare. She had only just been recalling his words and from the expression in his steady blue gaze she wondered if he was recalling them too.

There's no husband material in here for you.

She swayed with emotion, gripping the door frame for support. Seeing him there was like an arrow to the chest, but she did not want to show it.

He stood quickly and crossed, "Miss Highsmith, are you well?"

His hand reached for her arm, but she recoiled away, "I'm fine." she lied, "perhaps it was I who caught the sun today."

His brows furrowed, without thinking his ungloved hand gently felt her cheek and neck. Emma gasped at the feather-like touch. His hands were so big and yet his touch so gentle. She felt the ache within herself grow. It was a longing like she had never known before, as though her heart was trying to force its way out of her throat. She ached in other places too, more intimate places, places she had discovered as a teenager alone in her room at night. She'd never felt those places light up of their own volition before, it shocked her, embarrassed her beyond measure. The swell of her breasts rose and fell, her breath deepened as the back of Dewsbury's fingers brushed against her throat and then withdrew.

"You feel warm," he murmured. His eyes fixed on her mouth for what seemed like an age but could only have been a few seconds. "Allow me to escort you back to your rooms."

"No," she swallowed and his eyes followed the movement of her throat, transfixed. "I am well. I can manage on my own. Please return to your reading." Dewsbury looked confused for a moment, and Emma couldn't help but smile, "You're hiding then?" she asked.

He laughed softly, "Yes, I suppose I am hiding."

"Not doing a good job of it this time though," Emma replied, clinging onto any conversation that may distract from her yearning skin, "What, with the curtains drawn and the door propped open." She indicated his crude door stop, "Would Mr Bellinghan thank you for such abuse of his books?"

Dewsbury shrugged, a schoolboy-like innocence on his face, "From what I gather they rarely come to this wing of the house. I doubt he would even notice they'd moved."

"If it was too stuffy you could have always opened a window."

"It was not a draught I sought."

"Then what was its purpose?"

"To afford me a clearer audience of the private concert next door."

Her stomach rolled again, "Ah." She could not look up at him. She would not. The room began to spin. "I am sorry to disappoint. I had no idea I had an audience or else I might have played something more palatable. I was just...experimenting."

Her mind was screaming. Dewsbury was the only person in the world who knew that she had written that melody about him. Now he had heard her tortured, anguished version of it, what might he make of that? What was there to make of it even?

His fingers grazed her chin and ever so gently he lifted her head so that she was looking at him once again.

"What could those impossibly big eyes have found so fascinating about the floor I wonder?"

His voice was silky, an octave lower at least and seductive.

"N-Nothing," she choked, unsure, "I was embarrassed. I did not know anyone was listening."

"And yet it was still masterful."

His voice was barely above a rumble now. His index finger moved upwards to her mouth, seemingly of its own accord, and lightly caressed her bottom lip. He seemed closer than before. In fact they had both moved through the duration of their short conversation. Emma was no longer gripping the door frame for support, both she and Dewsbury had unconsciously moved closer together, drawn inexplicably together without either of them realising. She exhaled too deeply, her vocal chords tripped in the breath and she croaked a gentle exclamation. The sound shocked them both back to reality. Emma's cheeks burned with shame, whilst Dewsbury's eyes smouldered. He looked like he wanted to devour her right there in the library. What would happen if she reached for him now? Would he kiss her? Would it be heated and urgent, or tentative and slow?

She stepped away, "Please excuse me. I must..." and then she fled, leaving all unanswered questions in the doorway and did not look back.

Chapter 11

Emma woke flustered. She had had a restless evening alone in her room, having excused herself from dinner feigning a headache. Hannah had sent her up a tray of food, but she'd barely touched a bite, much to Tilly's disapproval. Emma had waved off her concerns, promising to eat a hearty breakfast instead. She lingered at the dressing table, prolonging the journey downstairs to a more Bellinghan-like time. She wanted to avoid Dewsbury and all those unanswered questions that had been uncovered in the library. She reflected that it had been exactly a week since she'd arrived at the hall. Only a week since she had met Mr Dewsbury. She laughed at the memory of that first meeting, the derision in his eyes, his instant dislike for her. That day in the music room, when he had come to apologise for speaking ill of her to Lydia, he had offered to explain the reason for his derision. Emma had declined to hear his explanation, thinking that he was grasping at excuses to avoid owning up to his rudeness. Now she wondered if it might have been better to have heard his tale. It may explain how they had gone from hating one another to wanting to devour each other in the span of a week.

Though she was a novice in matters of passion, she had come to recognise that on some level Mr Dewsbury did desire her. With hindsight she realised that he had always put himself in her path, even when he supposedly disliked her. The look in his eyes yesterday couldn't have been further from disinterest. She knew that he did not hate her, that he never really had. His recent gentlemanly conduct had proven that, but yesterday she saw something else. He hungered for her. It had been clear to see. She hungered for him too, but she would not risk her heart tasting something that could not be hers forever, and his desire for her did not promise a future together. If she was to live free as a spinster, then she could not carry with her regrets. She refused to be a jilted woman, forced onto the shelf by holding a candle for a man who would never make her forever his. It would be too painful, too humiliating, she had too much pride to concede to that. No, she had to ascertain his feelings clearly before anything more could proceed. Though how she was to do that she had no idea.

By ten o'clock her hunger could wait no more and she hurried down to the breakfast hall as quickly as she could manage. She found six of the eight Bellinghans enjoying their food, only Hannah and Will were missing.

"Emma, how are you feeling?" Charlotte asked, indicating a seat next to hers at the table. Emma took it gratefully, "Much recovered, thank you."

"Still no sign of our hosts?" asked Felicity, between sips of tea.

"I didn't pass anyone on the way here." Emma replied.

The Bellinghan wives all shared a knowing look.

Emma looked questioningly at Lydia.

"They must have found something better to occupy the morning with," she replied in her droll way.

Charlotte and Felicity cackled with laughter as their husbands exchanged their own exasperated looks. Just then the door opened, nine pairs of expectant eyes turned to seek the newly weds, only to find Mr Dewsbury enter the room.

Charlotte and Felicity deflated somewhat and returned to their meals. Emma felt the colour rise on her cheeks and looked away, while Lydia perked up considerably at the sight of her cousin.

"A bit late for you isn't it James?"

"Hush you, let the man eat." said Henry, crossing to Dewsbury and drawing him to the table, "Nice to see you with the rest of us James. You can stop putting us to shame with your early rising. You'll have to pack that in when you're Lord Dewsbury you know. No member of the peerage should be up before nine in the morning. It sends a bad message."

Dewsbury laughed and chose a seat next to Emma, "I will endeavour to change, for you Henry, and Lydia of course. I would not want to disgrace my esteemable cousin."

Henry laughed as he returned to his own seat to the right of his wife, "She'd managed that quite well enough on her own before I came along."

Emma's shocked eyes lifted to Lydia again, but her chaperone was too busy laughing and playfully swatting her husband with the back of her hand.

She felt Dewsbury's gaze on her before she turned and saw he was facing her, "Are you well, Miss Highsmith?" he asked gently.

"Yes sir," she replied, "I am well."

He looked to say something more, but then the door opened and at last their hosts joined the party looking flushed and in love.

"Here they are!" Cried Charlotte, "Oh, that newlywed life suits you both very well."

Hannah and Will merely grinned.

"Keeping up his end of the marital duty I see." Charles Bellinghan murmured to his wife, loud enough that those around the table could hear, but not so the happy couple could.

Emma and Dewbury both shifted uncomfortably.

Felicity scolded her husband, "My dear, you forget that it is not only family present."

He looked around the table, almost surprised to see Emma and Dewsbury sat there. His face fell with regret, "Oh my dear Miss Highsmith, do forgive my impertinence about my brother, I quite forgot that you are not a Bellinghan yourself, I've come to think of you as a member of the family this past week."

"I am not offended sir, please think nothing of it." But she mulled over the words as she tucked into her plate. 'Marital duty', she thought of that as the begetting of children, which she knew involved intimacies between man and wife that were too shocking to be spoken of to anyone outside of the medical profession. She did not know what it entailed, but she thought of Dewsbury's gaze from the evening before and her body's reaction to it. She saw Hannah's flushed cheeks, her languid movements and considered, for the first time, that it could be a thing that is enjoyable.

"A penny for your thoughts, Miss Highsmith?" Dewsbury's voice snapped her out of her revelry sharply. She should not be thinking of such things around the breakfast table.

"Nothing. No, n-nothing," she blushed, flustered and tittered nervously, "I was thinking about children. Hannah's children you understand. How I shall enjoy visiting to give music lessons. That is all."

The lie sounded hollow to her own ears, and yet Dewsbury pondered on it for a moment. "It'll not be long, I shouldn't wonder." He replied thoughtfully, "This house was built for children."

"Plenty of space." Emma agreed, glad to be moving on from her scandalous thoughts a moment ago.

"Yes, the bricks and mortar are generous enough, but I actually meant the family within. Look at them all," his eyes darted around the assorted Bellinghans, "they radiate love."

The sincerity of his words struck Emma so fiercely that she stared at him a moment. He looked earnest, and yet so sad that she felt obliged to give him some reassurance, "You will find that too, at the Elms, when the time comes."

He shook his head and looked down at his hands, a sad smile caught his lips, "I had the whole of the downstairs of the east wing remodelled to accommodate a large music room. Plenty of space for tutors and governesses. I thought of everything. Well, except…" he stopped abruptly, the unfinished sentence hanging in the air between them. The conversation had become too personal, they both knew they needed to change the subject.

"Will you dance at the ball?" Emma asked suddenly. They needed a new topic and it was the only thing she could think of.

"Not if I can help it," he replied smoothly.

"I know that is not because you cannot dance sir. I watched you dance with Hannah the other evening and you were most graceful."

"Graceful?" he exclaimed, some levity returning to his voice, "Only the other morning you were complaining about me lurking like some gargoyle."

"Well, two things can be true at the same time," she replied smoothly. That made him laugh, the noise of his chortle caught Lydia's attention who silently watched the rest of their exchange with interest.

"And will you dance Miss Highsmith? I have yet to have the pleasure of seeing that."

Emma sighed, "If past experience of public balls has taught me anything, then it is unlikely. Though I suspect I may have at least four Bellinghans added to my dance card this time, so that will be fun!"

Her voice did not betray any bitterness or resentment at the facts as she had laid them out. Though Dewsbury seemed insulted on her behalf at her treatment at other parties.

"Why will you not dance Mr Dewsbury?"

He sighed, "To dance would begin speculation about my being open to courtship. And I have no desire to have a whole ballroom full of scheming Mamas throwing daughters at me all evening."

"You are not open to courtship then?" Emma asked tentatively.

"Decidedly not," was Dewsbury's response, "It had been furthest from my mind when I first came here."

Emma quickly bit back her disappointment, "I hear that there will be many eligible young ladies in attendance," she replied, then added cheekily, "it seems cruel to deny them the opportunity to learn of your home refurbishments."

His eyebrows rose with amusement, "Now she mocks me! When a few kind words might have secured her a fifth name on that dance card."

Her insides shook, but her voice remained firm, "That would have been heroic indeed. Though it would have set a bad precedent. You said so yourself."

"So you do not want to dance with me?"

"I did not say that."

"You would refuse to dance with me?"

"To save you from those scheming Mamas."

"Now who's being heroic!"

"You said that you did not want people to speculate."

"I did say that." He conceded.

"You are not looking for a wife at the Ball."

"That had not been my intention, no."

Emma cocked her head and looked at him. His eyes danced merrily from their exchange.

"No?" she challenged. She was thinking of the afternoon yesterday, his hands around her rib cage, his finger touching her bottom lip. She wondered if he thought of it too, for his voice caught when he replied, "That had not been my intention."

There, she saw it, clear as day. The attraction between them was real, and mutual. It sparked between them with the ease of dry kindling catch alight. A smile engulfed her whole face, she could not stop it even if she'd wanted to. Dewsbury''s face lit up too.

"Will you ask me to dance?" she questioned.

He looked at her playfully, "Perhaps Miss Highsmith. Perhaps."

She laughed. If propriety would have allowed it then she would have playfully swatted him with the back of her hand just as she had seen Lydia do..

She shook her head and returned to her breakfast still smiling.

For the rest of the day Dewsbury did not leave her side, and the smile never left her lips .

Chapter 12

Miss Highsmith awoke the next day renewed and refreshed. Practically skipping out of bed she rang for Tilly and made her way downstairs as soon as she could. Today would be her last full day of complete freedom before the Ball. Her parents were due to arrive tomorrow evening to dine, she was already apprehensive about how Lydia would take to her Mama. More than that though, she was impatient to see Mr Dewsbury again. Yesterday had been wonderful. They'd spent the whole day together, he'd been so attentive, made her laugh and smile so much her cheeks ached. They'd discussed composers, instruments, concerts and compositions so much that Lydia had banned the topic of music during their evening dinner. After dinner in penance they had played another duet, sight reading the piece, making mistakes, fumbling their fingers together and giggling like children. Her head felt light with happiness, and the thought of their parting in three days time made her stomach clench.

Entering the breakfast hall she found him alone, her heart swelled at the sight of him. His face split into an infectious smile as he pulled out the seat next to his and she joined him, another day of blissful contentment ahead.

The day was filled with the usual activities, only each was made better by Dewsbury's constant companionship. That morning the whole group toured the woodland to the west of the house. They walked two by two, each lady accompanied by her corresponding husband, and Emma on Dewsbury's left arm, chatting and teasing as they walked. After luncheon the other ladies went to change, but Dewsbury and Emma stole away to the music room to work on a new duet. They sat too close, touched too often and laughed too loud the whole afternoon.

After dinner the hosts wanted to dance, and so the settees were moved aside and Emma took her place at the piano stool. Dewsbury danced with each lady, save one. Emma watched his graceful movements with envy. Between partners he would join her by the keys and turn the sheet music for her.

"My hero." she whispered to him in jest and watched his eyes dance. Intoxicating. She'd not touched a glass of wine all day and yet she felt drunk with joy. Mr Dewsbury had been right about the Bellinghans, they did radiate love, it was hard to not get caught up in it.

Captain Bellinghan had petitioned to dance with Emma, "Come now, seems only fair. I'm sure Felicity can butcher a country dance for us all."

That earned him a stern look from his sister-in-law.

Emma considered it for a moment, but dismissed the thought. She was still too nervous for them to see her dance. She was not a very physical person, she'd not had that many opportunities to improve her footwork, she felt awkward and alien on the dance floor. At the ball there would be lots of other couples and she'd be less of a spectacle. But here in the sitting room, it was all too intimate, she'd feel exposed. She refused his offer, insisting that she stay by the piano.

"I'll be filling in that dance card on Saturday though Miss Highsmith, make no mistake." The Captain had assured her before returning to his wife's hand instead.

Dewsbury had watched the exchange with some interest, but said nothing.

Before the night became too late Emma chose to excuse herself. The family looked as though they were far from ready to end the festivities, but she needed to rest if she was going to face her Mama tomorrow. Dewsbury offered to accompany her, and though this suggestion should have been refused outright by all parties, no one said a word.

Well, except Lydia.

"Take care of my ward, cousin." she slurred merrily, "No funny business."

Emma laughed. What a chaperone!

They walked in companionable silence until they reached the door of her bedchamber. Mr Dewsbury's rooms were further into the wing, but Emma had never ventured in that direction. She had no business to.

Turning to say goodnight to him, he surprised her by holding out his hand.

"Dance with me."

She'd blinked, confused, thinking she had missed part of a conversation, "At the ball? Of course."

"No, now."

She shook her head with misunderstanding, "Now? Here?"

He wrapped his hand around hers and pulled her gently into the centre of the corridor, "You haven't danced all week. That hardly seems fair. Dance with me now."

She stood across from him, "What if someone should see?"

He glanced down the empty hallway, "Who on earth might see at this hour?"

"There's no music."

"I'm sure you can think of something. What would you like to dance?"

"Cotillion."

He nodded in approval, "Can you think of a piece?"

"Yes."

"Then count us in."

He moved and stood opposite Emma. Even in this light she could see his blue eyes burning with intensity. What they were about to do would be considered scandalous, and yet she did not care a jot about that. She was more concerned about messing up the footwork.

"One, two, three, four."

They bowed to one another. Emma heard the music in her head distinctly, she let the tempo guide her feet.

Suddenly Dewsbury's hand was in hers again. She had not worn gloves in order to facilitate an evening of pianoforte and his had been discarded after dinner. His fingertips tickled her palm, her whole body felt it. They skipped towards each other, their bodies too close as his big arms encircled her as she turned. If they had danced as such in a public place they would have been shamed for the embrace, but neither drew away. They walked slowly in a circle, their eyes locked. His hands moved as they parted, she missed their warmth immediately. They surged closer again, turning as they paraded, their fingers interlocked too intimately for a real dance. Another turn, another parting and return. Again too close, too much bodily contact, too intimate.

By the end of their short set of steps they were both breathing heavily, and it had nothing to do with over exerting their muscles. The dance had barely lasted minutes, impossible to do more without the four other couples needed to complete the dance, and yet they both felt as though they had run a mile.They completed their bows to one another, only now Dewsbury stood apart from her and did not reach out. Perhaps he did not trust himself. Emma was convinced that if she moved closer they would quickly abandon even more rules than they already had that evening.

"You dance very well sir."

"And you. Nothing to be nervous about." His throat was dry and his voice husky. "Will you save the cotillion for me at the ball?"

Her heart hammered in her chest, "I look forward to it." And she did, she really did. "Good night Mr Dewsbury."

He smiled and bowed, "Good night, Miss Highsmith."

She watched him stride away as she gripped onto her bedchamber door handle for dear life. Emma blew out a breath before letting her head fall back onto the door with a thump.

A joyful laugh bubbled up from inside her chest, she let the sound fill the hallway for a moment, before turning the handle and finding her bed.

Chapter 13

She woke with a new sense of purpose. The ball was tomorrow evening and Dewsbury would dance with her in front of the entire assembly. Her heart skipped and her stomach churned as she thought about it. She'd never had higher expectations for a party than tomorrow evening, she wanted everything to be as perfect as it could be, and that meant keeping her mother as far from Dewsbury as humanly possible. They would have to be introduced today, there was no avoiding that. But if she could try and keep her away from him until the ball then she might save herself some mortification, lest her Mama attempt to 'help' her with her courtship. Mr Dewsbury would hate to be put upon, he'd see her as a scheming Mama, desperate to get her daughter's hands on his title. Despite the attachment that she and Dewsbury shared he had given her no reassurances of courtship. Everything between them was still so new and raw she was worried that her pushy Mama might scare him away. And he had spoken critically on several occasions about being targeting my marriage hungry Mama's.

Emma at least had the element of surprise on her hands. Her parents had no idea of Dewsbury's presence at the Hall, and even on acquaintance her Mama would not know about the title that would one day be his.

The men were all due to take their hunt that afternoon, which left Emma time to build up some resistance to Mr Dewsbury's charms. They had become too carefree, too openly intimate together these past three days. Her cheeks ached from their easy laughter. This was not something that she could exhibit in front of her mother, she had to retreat. Emma almost lamented her decision to not intervene with Hannah on behalf of her sisters. If she had managed to orchestrate an invitation for them then they would have been the centre of her Mama's attention rather than her.

Dewsbury's blue eyes sparked with joy as she greeted him later that morning. It was a little before eleven and she had entered the sitting room with Hannah and Charlotte. They were chatting amiably about the ball, but her eyes were always seeking that statuesque figure. She smiled at him, her heart glad to see him, her belly aching with longing. A look between them conveyed that they were both thinking of that illicit dance, those soft touches and gentle sighs. He was dressed for the hunt in a navy blue overcoat and white cravat. She had seen him on horseback of course, but never at a charge. She imagined him thundering through the park akin to Odin crashing into battle on his six-legged beast. Yes, that suited him well. There was more Viking warrior about him than Greek hero, though she did not know those tales as well. She would tell him that tonight before dinner and see how it would please him. The ladies were going to sit on the patio and wave off those brave hunters whilst they drank tea and bravely devoured all the biscuits. It was going to be a perfect afternoon.

Just then, a manservant entered and spoke to Hannah. Emma thought nothing of it, afterall her friend was the mistress of this house, she was drawn away to speak to servants often enough. But she caught Hannah making an exclamation of surprise, and all of the assembled party turned to look at her.

Hannah met her eyes, she looked a little crestfallen and sad for her friend.

"What is it?" Emma asked.

Hannah moved quickly over to her, taking her hands. "It would appear your parents have arrived early."

All the colour drained out of Emma's face, "But, but they aren't due until six this evening."

Hannah squeezed her fingers in support, "It would seem that they set off fashionably early."

Emma burned with shame at the effrontery of her mother, for this was her doing, of that she had no doubt.

"Hannah, I am so sorry, if you cannot accommodate them…"

"Of course we can accommodate them, we've room enough for an entire village. I can distract them with a long tour of the house perhaps, or the housekeeper can take them. We can find a solution. But they are heading here now, so perhaps…" she glanced from Emma to Dewsbury in a meaningful way.

"What is it?" he asked.

Emma started to move toward him, "Sir…" she began, before the door swung open and her parents were introduced to the room by the same manservant.

Hannah immediately switched into hostess mode, "Mr and Mrs Highsmith, what an unexpected pleasure to see you here so soon. Please, come and join us."

The usual bows were exchanged as Emma's Mama launched into her explanation, "The pleasure is all ours Mrs Bellinghan, but we have not been without our little Emma for so long, and she neglected to write for the entire week. Can you believe that! Having far too much fun here by all measures. But we missed her so much. I could not bear another moment without her. Could I, my dear?" She addressed the question to her husband, though gave him no time to reply, "You do understand Mrs Bellinghan? Or you will, one day, if you are blessed with children. You must forgive our intrusion." Her eyes alighted on Mr Dewsbury expectantly, assessing him greedily for something that Emma was ignorant of.

She had no idea how Dewsbury was taking this first introduction to her mother, for she dared not look at him. Despite her Mama's insistence that she missed her, she had not once looked at her daughter since stepping into the room. Her father crossed over to her though and kissed her on the cheek.

"It has been quite unbearable with you gone my love," he said softly.

Emma believed him, she was certain that her Mama would have spoken of nothing except what Emma might have been doing all week.

She moved now to her mother and pecked her on the cheek.

"Forgive me Mama, I have been much engaged here, as you said." She hated how feeble her voice had become.

Her mother scrutinised her for a moment, "But you look well Emma. The company has agreed with you. Your countenance is so much brighter than usual."

Her glittering eyes turned to Dewsbury again, whilst Emma's dropped to the floor. It was as though her Mama knew who he was already before they'd even been introduced, but how could that be? There's no way she could have known that there were any other guests present nor what he looked like.

"Allow me to make introductions." Hannah said, guiding the Highsmiths to meet Charlotte first. Her Mama made a few courtesy words to Charlotte, though they were short and quickly glossed over as she waited for Hannah to introduce the man standing near the fireplace. Emma did not cross over with them, she waited and watched the horrifying scene from across the room. She felt Charlotte slip next to her and squeeze her hand.

"Our other house guest Mr Dewsbury. As close to family as one can manage. Mr Dewsbury, Mr and Mrs Highsmith."

Mrs Highsmith hardly finished her curtsey before she launched into her pre-prepared speech. "So wonderful to make your acquaintance Mr Dewsbury. Of the Derbyshire Dewsbury's, I am to understand?"

Emma felt her stomach drop as she realised her mother knew exactly who he was.

Dewsbury's face hardened to granite, "You understand correctly madam," he replied.

"Your Uncle is a Duke I hear? How exciting! I do hope Emma has been affording you all the proper courtesies as a member of the peerage."

"I am not a member of the peerage madam. As you so rightly pointed out, it is my uncle who bears the title."

Emma felt sick.

"Oh indeed, indeed. I only meant, one day... " Her mother paused with a tactless twinkle in her eye, "well, one should not discuss such things."

"No. One should not." Dewsbury replies. His icy stare cut straight across the room to Emma. His face betrayed no emotion, but his eyes, his eyes betrayed rage. No, more than that. Hurt.

"And what have you learnt about my Emma since your stay here sir?"

"Mama!" Emma's blush ran from the crown of her head to the balls of her feet. She crossed over needing desperately to remove her mother from Dewsbury as quickly as possible.

"Pish, posh Emma. You cannot spend a whole week in a house with someone and not learn anything about them."

"Miss Highsmith plays pianoforte," was his bland reply.

Her mother's face fell, "Oh is that all." She turned and hissed at her daughter, "Please tell me you haven't been boring everyone with your incessant playing all week child?"

The words dried in Emma's throat. She wanted to protest, but felt herself withdraw back into that silent place inside.

Her mother ploughed on, "Anything else sir?"

"Perhaps you should ask someone else. Ah, here are the rest of the party now."

Sure enough the door opened and the other Bellinghans flooded in, chatting amongst themselves before they noticed the two new people in the room. Dewsbury took the distraction as an opportunity to slip away from and exit the room in the hubbub.

Emma watched him go, longing to go after him, to speak to him and apologise for her overbearing mother. But she was trapped, she would not be able to leave her parents all day.

The introduction to the rest of the party went as well as could be expected. Mr Bellinghan explained that the men were due to go out on a hunt and invited her father along. Once the men had departed Emma quickly suggested that they fetch the housekeeper to show her Mama to her room and then they would take a grand tour of the house. She reassured Hannah that her presence would not be needed as she must have many preparations to make for the ball tomorrow. It was a small lie, but Hannah still looked grateful. Emma lamented the peaceful afternoon of chatter and tea she would be missing, and now she'd never see Dewsbury tearing about on his horse like some Norse god. But one thing was very certain, for the next two days to have any chance of going smoothly: Mr Dewsbury and her Mama needed to be kept separate for as long as possible.

Chapter 14

Several hours later Emma was embarking on her second tour of Danford Hall. The men were at their hunt, the Bellinghan wives were on the patio enjoying the sun and here she was tailing after the housekeeper with her mother, being shown rooms that she had lived in for a week already. Still, anything was better than the potentially combustible combination of Lydia Bellinghan and her mother. Emma hoped they would be seated apart at dinner this evening. It was going to be bad enough with her mother and Dewsbury without throwing his cousin in the mix. Ah Dewsbury, the thought of him made her brow furrow. Why had he looked so betrayed? Why had he stared at Emma as though she was to blame? Her mother could be abrasive and crass, but that really wasn't Emma's fault. She had to try and get a moment to speak to him about this. That might be easier said than done, but she needed to know what she had done wrong.

"How many times do I have to tell you to stop squinting Emma. It will age you prematurely and Lord knows we don't need another impediment to you finding a husband."

"I thought you had finally given up on that idea Mama." Emma quipped back.

Her mother stopped dead in her tracks and turned to her, "My my, we have become brave. Why then, with this new found boldness, is the only unmarried gentleman in this entire house able to tell me nothing about you save you play pianoforte? He didn't even say you played it well."

Biting back her irritation Emma replied, "I came here to see my friend Hannah."

"Opportunities such as these do not present themselves often to women of your age Emma. You should have jumped at the chance to make a good impression. A Duke! He will one day be a Duke!"

"I did not know about that until later."

"How often are you able to be in the company of nobility? Foolish girl."

Emma felt like she was seventeen years old again and failing in her season in London. She had taken similar admonishments daily while they had been in town those long, unhappy months.

"How do you even know about that Mama?"

Her mother smiled with superiority, "Because your hostess did the honourable thing and wrote to inform me of their unexpected houseguest, I was curious about this Dewsbury fellow so I did some digging. She did not want me to think anything improper was going on. " Her mother snorted, "Chance would be a fine thing with you Emma! As if you could seduce him into marriage, but oh, a Dukedom! What a prize that would be for the family. Think of your sister's chances if that were the case!"

"What would you have had me do Mama? Throw myself at him for the sake of my sisters?"

"Nothing so rash! Just, try. Try to be agreeable to him. Do something, stop hiding in corners wishing to be anywhere else at the ball tomorrow."

Oh the irony, Emma had longed for the ball so she could stand up with Dewsbury in front of everyone. Now she dreaded the idea of exposing him to her mother's scheming.

"Have the other gentlemen indicated that they might ask you to dance?"

Emma nodded.

"Capital! Then he would be duty bound to ask you. I shall hint at it over dinner."

"I pray you do not Mama."

"Hush," her mother snapped. "All you have to do is smile, try and converse with him. Tell him how funny he is and how intelligent. Men liked to have their egos stroked as much as possible."

"I think he would hate that Mama."

"And what do you know of men? Nothing child, nothing. So you will do as I say and you can thank me for still taking an interest in your affairs despite your age. Your singular focus over these next twenty four hours is to get that Duke to notice you."

They rounded a corner and there, in the centre of the corridor, he stood. He was still dressed in his hunting gear and despite the warm weather his face was ashen and his stare cold. He met Emma's astonished expression for a mere second before he turned away and marched straight past both of them.

"Ah, Mr Dewsbury..." her mother gushed, but he did not pause. They listened to his thunderous steps for quite some time. Noise carried easily in these corridors, there was no way that he did not hear at least part of their conversation, though Emma had no idea at what point he might have caught it.

Her stomach swirled. He'd looked angrier then the first day they had met, she'd almost withered from his rage. She felt lost, as though she had somehow wiped out all of the connection they had built this last week in a matter of hours, but was unsure how. How could she remedy what she was ignorant of? She resolved to speak to him after dinner that evening, she had to know how to put things right, how to see the mirth in his eyes once again, and she'd have to do it away from her loud mouthed mother.

Chapter 15

The Bellinghan family always indulged in a spectacular dinner the evening before the summer ball. Hannah had outdone herself with the decor, the table burst with colour as elaborate flower arrangements rang the length of the mahogany banquet table.

"Violets and greenery, to symbolise first love and new beginnings," she explained to Emma as they took their seats. The mention of love made her eyes seek Dewsbury from across the room. Mercifully he had been sat away from her Mama, a blessing she was certain she could thank Hannah for.

"The Ball will follow the same theme?" she asked her friend.

"Yes, purples, greens, first love, new beginnings." Hannah's gaze also fell on Dewsbury. He had not spoken a word to Emma from the moment of her parents arrival, and he kept himself to himself. Everyone had noticed that he reverted back to his earlier brooding.

"I had meant to ask you Emma, what colour are you wearing tomorrow evening?"

Surprised by the question she met Hannah's gaze, "White. Is that alright?"

"Oh Em, yes of course it is, silly! You always look lovely in white, it brings out your doe eyes so beautifully."

Emma chuckled, "I never realised that my eyes were so big until this visit."

"Nor had I, until it was pointed out to me one evening."

Emma's heart thundered, "By whom?"

"Mr Dewsbury, while we were dancing a few evenings past. I joked and told him it must have been from all the exasperated eye rolls you did as you attempted to teach me pianoforte. Do you remember?"

The two giggled like school girls again. It earned Emma a disapproving look from her mother, which she ignored.

"I remember. You were hopeless, too busy thinking about your next romance novel."

Hannah's hands indicated the room around them and the people. Looking at her husband fondly she replied, "Now I live in one."

"First love," sighed Emma.

"And new beginnings," Hannah finished for her. "Now, I have a favour to ask. A silly little thing really."

"Of course, anything."

Hannah smiled, "I have convinced all our house guests to don something within the colour scheme of the ball. It's a bit a frivolity really, but they are all too scared to say no to me after I have worried so much after every detail. May I send some things up for you to wear? Anything would look good with white you see, and I'd like you to match the family as you are my oldest friend and esteemed guest."

"Hannah," Emma leaned forward and hugged her, "it would be such an honour to be included with your family. Thank you. This week has been heaven. Truly." To her astonishment she found that she was biting back tears.

"Gosh, I've missed you," she whispered into her ear.

Hannah squeezed her tight, "You never need to be a stranger to me Emma Highsmith, and you are welcome at Danford Hall anytime."

Both sniffing they parted just as the first course was served. Dabbing her eyes with the finger of her glove Emma glanced up to find Dewsbury looking over. Concern flashed across his features a split second before he looked away impassively. It had been the first time he had glanced at her with anything other than rage since this morning. It made her more determined than ever to discover the cause of his milaise. One way or another, by the end of this evening she would know why he was so angry with her.

THE OPPORTUNITY TO speak to him directly after dinner passed her by as he'd made it increasingly difficult to get anywhere near him all evening. He seemed to melt into shadows as soon as she approached, suddenly disappearing from her vicinity and emerging in some other part of the sitting room. Mercifully, he seemed just as adept at avoiding her mother, and neither Highsmith female managed to get anywhere near him all evening.

Felicity Bellinghan had begged Emma to play some music, much to the chagrin of her mother. She agreed to one song, and found herself alone at the pianoforte. There was no gallant blue-eyed giant to turn the pages for her this evening. It struck her that she would never again have his steadfast presence next to her. After tomorrow they would be strangers to each other. It was unlikely that their paths should ever cross again, they occupied very different social circles. Besides, he would be back in Derbyshire and she would be at home, living her little life on the dusty shelf. It was that thought that made her follow through with a very rash and unladylike plan.

Before ten she excused herself from the party, pleading fatigue. In truth she was far from tired and secreted herself in the corridor outside of her bed chamber and to wait patiently for Dewsbury in the dark of the guest wing. Desperation had motivated her into such a shameful action, but he had made any other approach impossible. Besides, the last time they had been alone together in this corridor he had enticed her to dance alone and unchaperoned, he could hardly claim innocence on unorthodox behaviour.

She waited a half hour in the dark until she heard his lumbered footsteps. He walked slowly with his shoulders hunched. His head was bowed and so when she stepped out to greet him he startled.

"Good God, what the hell!"

She ignored his curses, "My apologies Mr Dewsbury but I had to speak to you..."

"This cannot be borne Miss Highsmith. Please step back into your room."

"I will not."

"You will do as I ask. This is highly improper."

"You have been ignoring me all day," she took a small step towards him and the big man shrank away from her as though she might attack him. She stopped dead. "Dewsbury, please just tell me what is wrong."

His voice cut through the gloom like thunder, "Do not presume to address me in such a manner Miss Highsmith. There is no understanding between us that would give you the right to name me as such."

Now it was Emma's turn to step back, his words had struck her more painfully than any physical blow.

"My apologies sir."

He stared at her, his blue eyes dark and stormy in the low light, "Your Mama sent you, did she? I expect she is hiding round the corner waiting to catch us alone. What a pretty little scheme to entrap a peer of the realm. You women. You are all the same. I suppose she thought you were running out of time and decided to force the matter."

His voice was so bleak. Bitter, yes, but raw and broken. Full of despair. Had he not been so merciless, she might have reached for him to offer comfort.

"There is no scheme, no trap. Please believe me."

"Believe you? I heard the two of you scheming earlier! Your mother instructed you to catch my attention. To spend the next twenty four hours focussed solely on that in fact! But as I told you a week ago, I will not be caught. Now, good night."

"I never wanted to catch you," she heard the pleading tone of her voice, it was alien to her, it frightened her how much she wanted him to understand, "I didn't know about the inheritance. It means nothing to me. I wanted you. God knows why now. You were kind to me for a while. Your touch made me feel alive and I have been quiet for so long."

Too many words, too many feelings, but they gushed out of her, spilling her secrets for him to hear. And yet his expression never wavered from one of disgust.

"I do not believe you. From the moment we first met, despite my obvious disdain, you still stuck to your mission. Of course it all makes sense now. You were always after the money, why else would you seek out a man who so clearly disliked you. You used those brown eyes and extraordinary talent to bring me around. Such a pursuit! To manage me into marriage? It was neatly done Miss Highsmith. But it is over. I will not be manipulated any further."

Dumbstruck for a moment, Emma watched as he turned and walked further down the hallway. She did not reach for him, nor follow him in any way, but her voice pierced the quiet like an arrow, it stopped him in his tracks.

"Then you do not know me at all sir, nor yourself. It was you who sought me out. You were the one who pursued, not I. You took my hand and led me to dance, not the other way around. And what a merry dance that has turned out to be," she finished bitterly.

She could not tell anymore if he was facing her or not, but was certain that he was still there listening. She allowed the first tear to fall, many more were on their way and she had no wish to prolong this humiliation any longer.

"Good bye, Mr Dewsbury," she said.

Her voice was thick with emotion and she fled to her room locking the door behind her. Standing at the looking glass a moment, she gazed upon her devastated expression.

"Ah, there's the regretful spinster," she chided herself.

There was no music, no rush of notes to compose her feelings. All that was left was an emptying silence.

Emma Highsmith crumbled to the floor in a wave of sorrow.

Chapter 16

There was no need to feign illness to spare herself from having to join the others the next day, Emma had awoken from two hours sleep with a pounding headache. Her pillow was damp from her tears, she felt like a shadow of her former self. Tilly was shocked to see her charge so pale and drawn, she had insisted on sending for her mistress. Despite the early hour (by Bellinghan standards) Hannah had come at once.

"Em, my word what happened? Do you need a doctor? Drink this water."

"No please. Do not make a fuss for me. Perhaps I had too much wine last night."

Hannah frowned at the lie, while she passed her a glass, "I sat by you all night and you didn't have a sip. You wanted a clear head for the ball, you told me that yourself." She studied her friend closely, noting her swollen eyes, puffy cheeks and reddened nose, "You've been crying. Tell me at once what has upset you and I will make it right again."

Emma shook her head, "Please, don't do anything. It's your grand day. Don't let me spoil things."

"What use is a grand Ball when my oldest friend lies abed in pieces?" Hannah leant over and held her tight.

"You will have a thousand things to do today," Emma murmured into her cheek, "go and be fabulous Mrs Bellinghan. I will be alright, I will keep to my bed and rest until this evening. I look forward to seeing the grandeur later."

Hannah kissed her cheek briefly, "Shall I keep your Mama away?"

A wound, still new and raw, throbbed in Emma's chest at the mention of her mother. She nodded, her eyes brimming with tears. Concern spread over Hannah's expression but her friend waved her away.

"Go, you have too much to get on with."

"I will send you up some breakfast once the family are awake."

Emma thanked her, promised to rest and recover, told her how grateful she was to have such a caring friend, but an ungenerous sense of relief flooded through her once Hannah had left the room. How could she bear to see anyone else today, let alone pretend to make merry at the Ball? The thought of seeing Mr Dewsbury made her feel sick. Turbulent emotions swirled; dread, anger, sorrow, hurt all crashed together in the pit of her stomach. Add to that the humiliation, yes, the embarrassment at having misread his feelings so badly, of convincing herself that someone could have desired her when she'd always known in her heart that it was too late. She was a spinster now and forever, destined to sit on the fringes of society, never truly fitting in anywhere. Falling back onto the pillows more bitter tears fell.

An hour passed, The tears had dried, but she had not slept. How could she when, whenever she closed her eyes, her mind replayed every interaction she'd had with Mr Dewsbury in haunting detail.

A brief thud at the door warned her that she had a visitor incoming. She expected it to be Tilly, though the girl was never usually that loud, so sat up to see Lydia Bellinghan struggling through the door with a breakfast tray.

"Bloody door handle! Nightmare. How do the servants do it so gracefully? I'll ask Charlotte when I get a minute."

Dumping both herself and the tray onto the bed next to Emma she smiled knowingly at her ward, "You look like hell."

A laugh burst out of Emma unexpectedly.

Lydia approved, "Good, you're still in there. You look insensible. Eat and then we can talk."

"I do not think..."

"Eat," she commanded, "do as your chaperone says."

Emma did as she was bid, though she did warn, "I do not think you can still call yourself my chaperone now my parents are here."

"Your domineering friend then."

Lydia watched her closely as she finished a slice of toast, then passed her another glass of water, "Now this. All of it."

Emma rolled her eyes and finished it in four gulps. "Satisfied?"

Lydia appraised her carefully, "For now." She moved the tray to a bureau before returning to the bed. "Now, tell me what my idiot cousin said to you last night."

A flush glowed on Emma's cheeks as obvious as sunburn, "N-Nothing," Lydia looked unconvinced, "why do you ask?"

"Hannah tells me you're sick with tears and he's been acting even more of a bear than usual, and that's saying something. Now, given the attachment the two of you have so obviously made over the last week, it doesn't take a genius to put two and two together."

"There is no attachment." Emma looked miserable, "He told me that himself."

Lydia cursed, "Bloody fool. What else did he say?"

"He believes that I purposefully put myself in his path to ensnare him for his inheritance. Like an elaborately planned coup."

"Good god, he cannot believe that of you."

Emma shrugged, "That is what he said."

Lydia shook her head angrily, "I knew he was hurting, but I didn't think he was as damaged as all that. She's completely warped him."

"I don't understand."

She looked at her carefully, "He never told you about the circumstances by which he came to stay with Henry and I for so long?"

"Yes, The Elms is being remodelled."

Lydia took her hand, "Those works finished over a month ago Emma. He was too afraid to go back there and so he stayed on with us. He's always been so understanding and supportive of me despite... well, let's say, certain circumstances of my past, I'd let him stay with us forever if Henry could bear it. I never pushed him to return home because I figured that he knew his own feelings best. Now I see that was the wrong decision."

"Why would he not want to go home?"

"He commissioned the house remodel to accommodate his new wife. Two years ago, he was engaged to be married. The house was to be his gift to her, and the children they would raise together."

Emma's heart thud, "Oh," she replied blandly, "he loves another."

"Loved. Past tense. And, no, I don't think so. He was bowled over, swept up in her, but I think in time he would have seen her for what she was."

"What was that?"

"A schemer Emma. A shallow social climber. She only wanted him for his title, you see. She wanted to live life in London with the Ton, not raise children at The Elms."

"What happened?"

"She realised that our Uncle was in excellent health. Not due to die soon enough for Miss Raymond's tastes." Lydia snorted in disgust, "She wasn't willing to wait that long to be a Duchess. She found another young Lord to make her mark on. Left James in the spring and was married by the summer just as the house was finished. You've never seen a man so humiliated. It destroyed his trust in women. I thought he might never recover. When you first arrived here and I saw how he acted towards you, I was shocked at just how much she had damaged him. Your only crime in his eyes was to be unmarried, therefore you had to a gold digger and needed to be treated with suspicion."

Emma nodded, she remembered it well, "But then one day he changed. He apologised."

"And he became so attentive to you. I was overjoyed, it was like having the old James back after all these unhappy months. I was so pleased, I never wanted to see him go back to his behaviour before. I wonder what has changed?"

"My mother," Emma replied gravely, "he overheard part of a conversation in which she chided me for not making a big enough effort to impress the future Duke. I have not told her that we had made acquaintances during the week. She was advising me on how to throw myself in his path so he might ask me to dance at the Ball. The ironic thing being, he had already requested a dance! She just didn't know it." Emma sighed, "He believes me to be a fortune hunter?"

"No, of course he doesn't. Not really." Irritation flooded Lydia's tone, "He's let his idiot brain get in the way of what he knows in his heart. He was hurt in the past, he has vowed to never let that happen again, to protect himself, but he's reading signs that aren't there and jumping to conclusions. We Dewsburys have a family history of that, you know."

"What can I do?"

"Are you sure you want to do anything? He has treated you abominably. Serve him right to be heartbroken a second time."

Emma looked down at her hands and said quietly, "I want to love him, I believe the process has already started."

Lydia squeezed her hand, "Oh my dear. I was hoping you would say that."

She thought for a moment, "You just need to show him somehow that it was real. In his heart he knows it already, he just needs to move through these idiotic fears. Make him certain that you like *him*, not his money. Then, when all is well and he is fawning all over you, you make him grovel like the dog he is for making you feel so wretched."

Another tear fell, only this time there was no sorrow.

Lydia wiped it away with her thumb, "Now then, no more of that. You need to eat that plate of food and drink that entire jug of water.

We've got all day to get you ready for tonight, and I can't have you looking like some bedraggled corpse, it would reflect badly on me as your chaperone."

"Domineering friend," Emma corrected with a smile.

Lydia put her arm around her, "With any luck, after this evening I'll be so much more."

Chapter 17

Emma remained in her room for the rest of the day, though she was rarely alone. Periodically she would have a Bellinghan visitor, each of the wives visited her to keep her abreast of the business happening downstairs.Mr Dewsbury was largely absent she was informed. Emma could picture him lurking in the gloom of the private library, with nothing but a brandy bottle and his pride to keep him company. Was he happy he'd pushed her away? Was he more content now he'd removed himself? She doubted it. He had seemed to come alive these past few days, just as she had. He'd been animated, enthusiastic and playful with the group. Lydia had said that that was the cousin she remembered from before his heart break. His dark and brooding presence from ten days ago was a long-term symptom of his ailment, and Emma had been the cure.

How could she convince him that her feelings for him were real? She had no idea, but she was going to try. Her whole future happiness might depend on her finding the courage to speak to him again. She was afraid, yes, the little mouse had returned. But she had to find the strength to be a lion this evening, and she would. She'd been twenty five years on this earthly plane and never once came close to love, now it was within reaching distance, and she was ready to grab for it with both hands.

BY FIVE O'CLOCK ALL the ladies were in their chambers preparing for the Ball and the wondrous evening ahead. As Tilly fussed around with curling tongs and pins Emma stared at her reflection and wondered how Hannah was feeling. She wanted everything to go well for her tonight, to quiet any gossiping tongues who dared suggest that Hannah Clayton was not a worthy wife for William Bellinghan.

A young housemaid entered carrying a small parcel. Tilly smiled as she approached, "From the Mistress?"

The girl nodded, presented Emma with the package and then departed.

"Open it Miss, open it!" Tilly squealed.

Caught up in her frenzied excitement Emma giggled too.

"What is it Tilly?" she asked as her fingers unravelled the string and paper. A black velvet box was revealed. A jewellery case, it had to be.

Emma gasped in surprise, "Why has Hannah sent me this?"

"For the theme!" Tilly squealed, "Oh do open it Miss, I'm dying to see what she's sent."

Emma gingerly popped open the gold clasp and the two women held their breaths as she opened the box. Never in her life had Emma been presented with jewellery before, she gazed on the set with wonder. Eleven glittering penny sized amethysts sparkled from the box, each was set on a silver hair pin. Their bright violet hughes mesmerised Emma for a moment. Between them lay a necklace. Thirty oval shaped amethysts, graduated in size, sat in silver settings that linked together tightly.

The two dumbstruck women stared. Emma had never even seen an amethyst before, let alone worn one. For many years it had been a stone that only the royal family could wear due to its rarity and deep purple colour. She blinked back tears.

"Here Miss," whispered Tilly, in reverence to the jewels, "there's a note."

With shaking fingers Emma opened the small envelope. It read:

To my darling Emma,

These stones have travelled all the way from South America to be with you tonight and forever. They are our gift to you to say thank you for adventuring at Danford Hall and entertaining us with your spectacular talent at the pianoforte.

I'm only sorry I was not a better pupil!

Wear them tonight to symbolise serenity, clarity and deep love.

My fondest regards, always

Your friend,

Hannah Bellinghan

Emma let out an audible whimper.

Tilly nudged her gently, "Oh, they'll look wonderful in your dark hair Miss. Though eleven is a funny number, don't you think? Not to worry though, Tilly will make you look like a goddess tonight."

And Emma believed her, she truly did.

Chapter 18

Guests began arriving in their droves, and by eight o'clock the Hall was abuzz with life. The Bellinghan family stood to receive each one, but Emma was free to wander around gawping at the grand flower displays, tables of exquisite food and, of course, the dazzlingly dressed guests from the Bellinghan social circle. Though, Emma caught more than a few glances her way, which was a novelty to say the least. The jewels in her hair and around her neck seemed to catch the light wherever she went. She was wearing her best white satin ball gown with long white gloves, but Hannah had also sent violet silk ribbons which Tilly had tied around the waist of the gown. She'd even fashioned tiny bows and tacked one to the top of each of her gloves. Tilly's magical hands had conjured her straight chestnut hair into tight face framing ringlets and an elaborate chignon at the back. Then, she had carefully placed the eleven amethyst pins throughout the style. Oh how she had fussed over their placement! But it was worth it. Emma felt more beautiful than she had in her entire life.

Hannah and Will had been so busy that she had not had a chance to thank them yet for their gift. Mr Dewsbury was nowhere to be seen. She wondered if she would have to scare him out of hiding. She saw her parents approaching and her heart sank. She'd be duty bound to stay with them for most of the evening.

Her mother looked her over with an astonished expression, "But where did you get those jewels?" she asked, agog.

Emma explained about the colour scheme and the gifts. Her Mama sniffed, "We were not sent anything, were we Mr Highsmith?"

Her father patted her hand, "I rather suspect my dear, that the honour was only extended to Mrs Bellinghan's very best friends, and neither you or I can claim that sort of acquaintance with her." He assessed his eldest daughter closely, "You look splendid, my love."

"Thank you Father."

"You are recovered from your illness this morning?"

"Yes, thank you."

"We must find you someone agreeable to dance with this evening," said Mrs Highsmith, eyeing up the other guests.

Emma took a deep breath, "Mama, I will not be persuaded to pursue Mr Dewsbury despite what you..."

Her mother flapped her hand, "Oh no my dear. He is the rudest man I have ever met. Why he's hardly said three words to me this whole time I've been at Danford. No wonder you struggled with that one. No, no." Her Mama took her arm, "You look like a princess tonight, let us find you another, more agreeable young man to speak to."

Emma's heart squeezed; it was the first compliment that her mother had given her since she had first come out into society eight years ago

.

The three of them circulated the rooms for a time, speaking to no one but themselves. They weren't acquainted with anyone, and there was no one available to introduce them, so they had to satisfy themselves by observing the distinguished guests. Eventually they were approached by Hannah's brother George and his wife Penelope Clayton. The Clayton's were their neighbours and had become acquainted with William Bellinghan when, in his role of Magistrate, he investigated a highway robbery that the Claytons had been victims of. That was how Hannah and William had met over a year ago. Emma always thought it sounded like the plot of one of those romance novels Hannah was always tearing through. She really did live in a fantasy.

The announcement of the dancing came not too long after. Everyone crowded in the Ballroom to watch the whole Bellinghan family begin the festivities. All eight of them looked regal and happy. How four brothers had managed to find such compatible partners was beyond Emma's comprehension. Each wife provided the perfect foil for her respective Bellinghan, and the four women together were a joyful combination. Emma would miss each of them she realised. It really had been a very happy week...with one noticeable exception. As if on cue she finally caught sight of Mr Dewsbury. He was quite easy to find in the crowd, being so tall he towered above most of the other guests. He stood on the opposite side of the dancefloor, watching his cousin complete the quadrille. He wore black evening wear with white gloves and a white cravat. But in the candlelight she caught a glimpse of a jewelled cravat pin, it was an amethyst set in silver, in exactly the same shade as hers.

Her eyes wandered to the Bellinghan family members. Each couple wore matching jewels but they all wore shades of green, only Dewsbury and herself wore amethysts. The two of them weren't Bellinghans she supposed, but Hannah had ensured that they were meant to be seen together, a couple, a matching pair just like the others. Eleven hair pins, she'd been sent eleven penny sized amethysts that sparkled in the light. Tilly had said eleven was an odd number, Emma would be able to tell her now where the twelfth one went- she was looking at it in Mr Dewsbury's cravat. She smiled..

Oh Hannah, you are still a romantic at heart.

As if sensing her attention was on him, Mr Dewsbury met her gaze. She had not seen him since he had accused her of being a fortune hunter, but she thought some of the venom had left him, though it was difficult to see for certain at this distance. She glanced away thinking of how difficult the situation was this evening. How could she possibly approach him alone when he was convinced that she was trying to entrap him? Trying to get him alone would surely only confirm his suspicions, but then how could she speak to him if not in private? The whole thing seemed impossible. She dared another look at him, but he was gone. Of course, crawled back to his hiding place. She felt a stab of irritation. It was like those early days of their acquaintance all over again.

The crowd jostled slightly and she felt someone standing very close. Looking up she found, to her surprise, Mr Dewsbury stood to her left. His eyes never left the dancing but he stood so close that she could feel the solid warmth of him against her bare upper arm. Rather than igniting excitement in her, she found herself rather antagonised. She took a step forward, escaping away from the contact, but then a few seconds later he was there again, at her side.

Angry now, she found her foot tapping beneath her gown. It was a frantic tempo and in her mind crashing chords bounced around like marbles.

The Bellinghans completed their dance, each man bowing to his wife and offering his arm as they guided their radiant wives off the dancefloor. It seemed like a good time to try and thank Hannah and William for their generous gift, so Emma began moving away from the ballroom to follow her hosts. She was stopped by a hand on her elbow.

"Miss Highsmith," Mr Dewsbury bowed, "may I enquire after your health?"

Incised at his gall, Emma felt bold, she did not curtsey back, "I am well. Now if you'll excuse me, I think I saw a Viscount in the next room who, naturally, I am planning to ensnare. Good evening."

She turned but did not manage to complete a step before his hand brought her back around to face him. His eyes twinkled playfully, they always seemed to whenever she challenged him. But she was in no mood for games. He had insulted her deeply, he'd made things impossible between them. Even though her plan had been to show empathy for his past, his behaviour last night had hurt her deeply, just for a moment she wanted him to know that.

"Please do not presume to touch me sir. There is no understanding between us that would give you the right to handle me as such." She indicated his hand on her elbow as she threw his own words back at him.

Dewsbury looked as though he had been struck, "My apologies Miss Highsmith."

He swiftly removed his hand, then mumbled, "I simply wanted to ascertain that you are well."

Emma gestured to herself, "As you see."

"Yes. Yes I see, you look very well."

A pause crept between them. More was to be said, but neither knew where to begin. Emma was still rattling through angry emotions when she caught her Mama gesturing to her. Mr Dewsbury must have truly fallen from her mother's good graces if she would not even approach him now. This amused her somewhat.

"Good evening sir."

She did not wait for a reply and strode confidently away, though inside she felt anything but conviction. What had she done?

OVER THE NEXT TWO HOURS she had little time to dwell on her interaction with Mr Dewsbury, not when there were four Mr Bellinghans on her dance card. Despite her reservations about dancing in front of a crowd of people she felt no unease as she skipped and laughed through every step. She was not under scrutiny from any of the other guests, how could she be when none of them knew her and she only danced with married men? She was beyond their notice, and this unburdened her. She found herself thinking perhaps the life of a spinster would not be so bad after all.

She'd just finished a lively country dance with Henry and the two of them had walked over to the refreshments area to speak to Lydia. At their requests, Henry dutifully fetched a lemonade for Emma and a glass of champagne for his wife.

"What on earth have you done to my cousin?" Lydia asked animatedly.

"What do you mean?"

"He's been watching you all evening. I really thought he'd have gone back into hiding by now."

Emma looked around, she could not see him anywhere, "I had not noticed."

"No, of course you haven't, you've been too busy having fun, which is exactly as it should be. Have you approached him at all? Spoken to him?"

"No... That is, I did not approach him, he approached me."

Lydia's eyes glowed, "Fascinating. What did he say?"

"He came to enquire about my health. He'd obviously heard about my ailment this morning."

"Oh, he's been plaguing me about it all day."

"Has he?" Emma squeaked.

"Oh yes. Every twenty minutes 'is she well Lydia? Is she well?'. I almost snapped at him, reminded him to think of why you might possibly be upset."

"I'm afraid I was rather short with him too."

Lydia beamed with pride at her protege, "Interesting. Well done Emma! Time for a little experiment I think."

Perplexed, Emma knew better than to try and dissuade her ex-chaperone and so watched bemused as she called Captain Bellinghan over and, a few moments later, he was introducing her to a very dashing looking Lieutenant Fox. He had an easy going nature and a wicked grin. They spoke for a good ten minutes about Bach. The Lieutenant had some interesting opinions about the depth of his work, to which Emma was more than happy to correct him on. He took it all in good humour, and she felt proud at the ease in which she had conversed with him. Since she was already amongst friends she found meeting him a trifle. When he had enquired about her dance card though Emma had flushed and some of her usual shyness returned.

"I see you have the cotillion free," he remarked, "it is coming up next, may I have this dance?"

"I believe you owe me that dance Miss Highsmith," Dewsbury remarked, materialising out of nowhere.

She assessed him closely, he seemed tense.

"It is true that Mr Dewsbury had asked for that dance a few days ago," she was speaking to the Lieutenant but her eyes never left Dewsbury's face, "but I was unsure if Mr Dewsbury was willing to keep to that request."

"Allow me to prove it to you then Miss Highsmith."

He held out his arm to her. Hesitating for just a second, she took it. Her fingers wrapped around his forearm and he walked her to the floor. Both of them forgot to bid goodbye to the Lieutenant, it was as though he had never existed.

As they reached the dancefloor and took their places, Emma became aware that this time she had caught the attention of a number of strangers. The eyes of the matchmaking Mama's and single debutants all flew to the floor to watch Dewsbury stand to dance. Ironically, her own Mama was not amongst them.

She felt a prickle of nerves, though it was too late now, she would not back out.

"Are you sure you want to do this sir?" She asked him haughtily, "Won't this open up speculation about you finding a wife?"

The music began and they bowed.

"There is no need to speculate," he replied.

Their hands touched, gloved this time, but the familiar steps brought to mind the memory of their silent evening dance. Emma felt a swell of emotion.

"Miss Highsmith, Emma, please let me apologise for what I said to you last evening."

They turned and parted, then came together again hand in hand.

"Yes, you should, you were a beast."

"Yes, I am all those things you have named me; a beast, a gargoyle, a ghost. A shade of my former self."

They turned again.

She met his eyes, "Lydia told me, about Miss Raymond."

"Ah." His complexion flushed with emotion, "She wounded me, perhaps deeper than I appreciated, though I will not use that as an excuse. I know you have no interest in excuses."

Her lips curved into a shy smile. He took it as a good sign and continued, "I should never have let my fear cloud my judgement of you Emma. We have not known each other for very long, but I know what I said to you was not a fair reflection on you, or your mother."

"Well, I don't know about that last part," she replied.

He laughed as they parted again. When they came back together she added, "I did not know, about the inheritance I mean. It means nothing to me."

He shook his head, "It matters not. I believe you, but it matters not. What I know to be true is what you said to me yesterday; it was I who approached you. You did not try to ensnare me, I wanted to capture you. I cannot think how, in my blind rage, I could have overlooked that. You must think me a fool."

"Yes," she laughed, "and I suppose I am one too for wanting to forgive you so very much. A wiser woman would have strung it out I'm sure."

"So, you forgive me?"

"Of course."

He beamed and held her closer, much closer than society would deem proper. He lowered his lips to her ear so that only she could hear what came next, "I do not think I can be without you now Emma. I could not abide another day without your company. You said that I brought you to life, well the same can be said for you. I was alone with my brooding for so long I never thought I'd leave, until you came and threw open the curtains. I want to sit and listen as you teach our doe eyed children to play pianoforte."

"In the east wing at the Elms?" she asked coyly.

"I'll be there to turn the pages," he murmured, so close now that she could feel the tickle of his breath on her ear.

A shiver ran through her body, "My hero," she whispered.

The music had stopped. Reluctantly they parted and bowed to each other. A murmur built around the room at their scandalous closeness, though she couldn't have cared a jot, she only had eyes for Dewsbury.

He offered her his arm, "I think there is more to say Miss Highsmith."

"Yes," she croaked.

"Perhaps I should meet you in the music room, say in ten minutes time?"

"Yes," it was a whispered longing, it quivered in the air between them like the final chord of a symphony. His blue eyes ignited at the sound.

He walked her to the edge of the ballroom before separating himself reluctantly and disappeared through the crowd.

Emma sought Lydia, explained that she needed to excuse herself and tried to ignore Lydia's knowing wink as she quietly slipped out of the party to hurry away.

Chapter 19

Emma paced nervously in the darkened music room. Her heart was pounding with anticipation; waiting for Dewsbury, each second felt like an hour. Her fingers itched, being so close to the pianoforte was another torture, eventually she could take no more. Practically ripping open the lid to access the keys, she threw herself onto the piano stool and launched into a frenzied improvised melody. She became so engrossed after five minutes that she almost didn't notice the door open and Mr Dewsbury entering holding a candle. The orange light lit his strong features and she was once again reminded of his statuesque qualities. Her fingers slowed as she adjusted to his presence, the melody slipped into something more melodic, calm and dream-like. The music of a contented soul rather than the frantic tempo she'd been playing a moment before. Resting the candle on top of the lid, he came to sit with her at the keys. He did not say anything, nor did he interfere with her playing. He just sat and listened. Emma was not certain what it was she was supposed to do in such a situation. She had agreed to the liaison without much thought after all. She knew what she wanted to do, to take his face in her hands and kiss him till her lips ached, but bold as she had felt at times that evening, she was still a little shy mouse underneath. So, she sat, she played, she enjoyed the feeling of him next to her, leant on him a little and felt herself held up by his strength. Her face dipped to her left and she leant her cheek on his shoulder. She felt his satisfied moan as she rested there. The rumble in his throat vibrated her cheek. Closing her eyes she took in the scent of him, musky and masculine. His arm slipped around her, his fingertips resting at her hip and he snuggled her in closer. Somewhere she had stopped playing, she was listening to the music of his heartbeat and steady breath instead.

"Emma," he spoke in a rumble, in a voice newly awakened from a long sleep, "will you be my wife?"

She sat up and looked at him. That was a mistake, the only thing holding them back from one another had been the lack of eye contact. Within a second they leant to close the space between them and his lips claimed hers in a long lingering kiss. He leant his forehead on hers, his breath hitched, "You haven't given me an answer."

She kissed him again, her hand finding the back of his head and drawing him closer. She wasn't certain about what to do, but the previous kiss had sent waves of pins and needles all over her body. She wanted more, no, *needed* more of that feeling everywhere. She needed him everywhere.

He whined her name into her lips, "Emma!" he pleaded, still seeking for his answer.

"Yes," she breathed, consenting to everything, anything he could give her, "yes, in every way yes."

That was all the encouragement he needed. His hands moved to capture her face and he drew her in further, teasing her mouth with his own, encouraging her to open up and move with him. She followed his lead, enjoying immensely the surprising tenderness of his mouth. Shocked at the softness of his lips and the growing need within her to not let this end, to demand more and more of what he was giving her. His mouth moved to kiss her chin, her cheek, her neck. When he kissed a spot just beneath her ear she felt a shudder of pleasure overcome her, like being submerged in a gloriously warm bath. A ragged moan slipped out of her lips at the flood of sensation, she blushed at the sound of her own wanton desire, her whole body felt alive. Between her thighs throbbed, it demanded attention as Dewsbury kissed her there again, ran his tongue to her earlobe and nibbled. She arched her neck, inviting him in further, encouraging his exploration. She arched her back too, her breasts pushing further into his chest and he kissed her throat and sent spirals of fire through her skin. It was not enough, not nearly enough. She needed more. Scooping both hands around his neck she stood briefly before swinging her leg over his lap and straddled him on the piano stool. Dewsbury's eyes flashed with surprise and delight in the candlelight. She needed to feel some pressure on her crotch, it ached and throbbed with the need to be touched, to be pressed against something. Only once she was fully pressed against his lap did she find some relief. His arms encircled her, encouraging her to lean fully into him, and there she discovered the extent of his arousal, thick, hard and perfectly positioned to offer her some succour.

"James," she moaned into his lips and felt his smile before he kissed her again, before his hands moved to her backside, before he rocked her forwards and revelled in the sound of their choked exclamations.

Yes, indeed, they made much music that night at Danford Hall.

Epilogue

Two Years Later
Derbyshire, England, June 1816

DISCORDANT NOTES FLOATED through the east wing of The Elms. Emma hurried down the corridor towards the music room not wanting to miss a moment. A joyful squeal filled the air as more keys were mashed under those beautiful star shaped hands. Those chubby fingers were always exploring, always grasping for new experiences without any fear.

She heard James laugh, "Not so hard young man, otherwise your mother would kill me."

Pushing the door open gently she stood in mock surprise at seeing them both sat at the piano stool, side by side, her blue eyed boys, one big and one (for now at least) small.

She gasped, "What are you doing at my pianoforte Colin Dewsbury? Are you making mischief or music?"

"A little of both I think," replied James with a smile.

Emma's heart squeezed as it always did when he looked at her like that; like she was the only thing in the entire world that mattered.

"What's that you've got?" he asked, indicating the envelope of crested paper she was holding as he bravely battled their son climbing all over his lap trying to escape to his mother.

"An invitation to the Bellinghan summer ball."

Colin had succeeded wriggling free of his father and ran towards her, his kness kicking wildly up in the air as he charged towards her skirts. She scooped him up into her arms and he squealed again as she marched him back to his father.

"Good Lord, is it that time of year again?" asked James as she took her seat next to him and passed him the squirming child.

She hummed as she tinkled out a little tune on the keys, it was light, youthful and upbeat, full of hope and exuberance.

"Yes indeed," she replied, then turned to look at him playfully, "the question is, are you ready for another adventure at Danford Hall?"

A now familiar look filled his eyes and a thrill of excitement ran through her whole body.

"With you my love, I am ready for endless adventures."

Emma smiled at her husband, leant forward and kissed him slowly as their son smacked his hands enthusiastically onto the pianoforte keys.

Don't miss out!

Visit the website below and you can sign up to receive emails whenever Jeanne Johnson publishes a new book. There's no charge and no obligation.

https://books2read.com/r/B-A-FDTX-CNRDD

BOOKS 2 READ

Connecting independent readers to independent writers.